Hush, My Darling
Leigh Kenny

Sister Creep Press

Copyright © 2024 by Leigh Kenny

All rights reserved.

No part of this publication may be reproduced, distributed, or transmitted in any form or by any means, including photocopying, recording, or other electronic or mechanical methods, without the prior written permission of the publisher, except as permitted by U.S. copyright law. For permission requests, contact the author.

The story, all names, characters, and incidents portrayed in this production are fictitious. No identification with actual persons (living or deceased), places, buildings, and products is intended or should be inferred.

Cover Art: Christy Aldridge at Grim Poppy Design

Edited by: Danielle Yeager, Hack & Slash Editing

Format Images: LM Kaplin

Interior Formatting: Leigh Kenny

First edition 2024.

Praise for Leigh Kenny

"As evidenced by her dazzling debut, Cursed, Kenny is a bright new voice in modern horror, one that is poised to take the genre by storm."

Kealan Patrick Burke, Bram Stoker Award-winning author of Kin and Sour Candy

"Kenny weaves a story of terror in the untamed wild, where the line between reality and nightmare blurs together as one."

M L Rayner, best-selling author of Echoes of Home

"Kenny's sophomore outing proves her aptitude for scaring us, and her range as a storyteller. Hush, My Darling is a harrowing tale of human monsters, their twisted view of the world, and the perpetual damage they leave in their wake. It's part Deliverance, part Wrong Turn, and part Texas Chainsaw Massacre."

Ben Young, author of Stuck and Home

"A potato wrote this, and it's f**king incredible!"

Mike Salt, author of the Linkville Horror Series

"I loved Cursed, but Hush, My Darling is something else entirely."
Sarah Jules, author of FOUND YOU and DON'T LIE

"Leigh Kenny's eloquent use of prose gave me an existential crisis about my own process!"
C S Jones, author of Colours

"Chilling and terrifying, Cursed is an expertly written tale from a new voice in horror. Do you dare take the box?"
Jay Bower, author of Cadaverous and The Terror of Willow Falls

"Kenny's gripping horror, infused with emotional depth, will leave readers both terrified and deeply moved."
B C Hollywood, author of The Darkle Chronicles

"It's no wonder Kenny is a rising star in the world of horror, her vivid storytelling and natural ability to seamlessly weave razor-sharp tension with spine-tingling dread make her one to watch."
Elizabeth J. Brown, author of The Laughing Policeman

"Kenny's latest shows just how versatile her writing skills are. Hush, My Darling takes a hard turn away from the spooky, creepfest that was Cursed, and instead explores the terror of an everyday threat; those who are born to cause others harm."
MJ Mars, author of The Suffering

"I can count on one hand the number of debut authors who've piqued my curiosity like Kenny has with her unique perspective and the promise of a new reign of unapologetically authentic terror. Let the bodies hit the floor, Leigh."

Nick Roberts, award-winning and best-selling author of The Exorcist's House and Mean Spirited

Content Warning

Hush, My Darling is an Irish horror thriller that delves into the depths of human resilience... and human cruelty. This book contains scenes of horror that some readers may find upsetting.

It also contains British English spelling and grammar, which some readers may also find upsetting.

For my mother, the strongest woman I know.

***

Here's to strong women.
May we know them,
May we be them,
May we raise them.

This inhuman place makes human monsters.

Stephen King

The caged bird sings with a fearful trill
Of things unknown
But longed for still . . .

Maya Angelou

Prologue: Lauren Screams

Through glassy eyes, she stared at peeling wallpaper.

Once upon a time, it had probably been a lovely shade of something, but the colour had long since bled from the paper, the delicate floral pattern in a multitude of brown shades barely discernible from the weeping damp patches. As the naked light bulb see-sawed over her head, she forced herself to focus on the spot where the paper curled just so.

That was where she had hidden herself.

They wanted to break her, body and spirit, and she knew that they were probably much closer to achieving their goal than they realised, but still, she needed to keep a little piece of herself safe from their dirty, calloused hands and hot, putrid breath.

A silent, solitary tear traced a path down one cheek. It stung where her flesh was broken. Stung where her mind was broken, too, so she continued to concentrate on that innocuous curl of tattered paper.

Lauren was gone now. Nothing more than an intricately fashioned name on a delicate silver chain that rested within the walls of her prison. Her name was the only thing she had left, and yet she chose to let it go, secreted away in the crumbling cinder wall, closer to touching the outside world than she ever would be.

Goodbye, Lauren, *she thought, a small, sad smile cracking her parched lips. As old wounds reopened, she could taste the tang of blood.*

SMACK!

"What the hell are you smiling about, girl?"

She was still reeling from the blow. Stars danced as the room reduced in a vignette. With a grunt, he rolled off her, the mattress groaning beneath his bulk.

"You don't smile unless I give you permission to smile, you hear me, darlin'?"

Spittle flew from his mouth speckling her face, brown-tinged globules as bitter as the look in his eyes. His cold, hard gaze locked onto her. She stared back, unflinching.

There was nothing left that he could take. Nothing for her to fear.

Death, *said her mind.*

But she didn't fear it.

She knew she would welcome its dark embrace after all she had endured at the hands of these animals. They were nothing more than monsters masquerading as men.

With a deep, phlegmy growl, he pulled back and spat a brownish glob of something onto her bare chest. As he stood looking down at her, she couldn't tell if the glint in his eyes was cruelty or lust. It was probably both.

It was always both.

She hoped with all her being that he wouldn't command her to rub the disgusting mucus into her chest like the last time. It had been horribly degrading, even by his standards, and it had only served to excite him, which never ended well for her.

To her relief, he picked up his ragged jeans from the floor and left the room without another word.

As the door thumped closed and the key turned in the lock outside, relief flooded her bruised body.

After her arrival, it hadn't taken long for those particular sounds to signify safety, however temporarily. To hear them in the opposite order, though . . . well, they were just about the worst sounds she had heard in her life.

If she ever escaped this godforsaken place, those sounds would haunt her for the rest of her days.

Who was she kidding?

She was never getting out of here. Sixteen good years had been all she got before her world was snatched away, and she knew she needed to make her peace with it. She would die here.

She already had.

It was only a matter of time before they brought her to the basement. She had heard them talking about it. They hadn't even bothered to whisper or mask their words. Why would they mask their words when they had never bothered to mask their intentions?

There was another girl down there. She had heard her screams. It had been so difficult to block them out, but it was getting easier. She wasn't sure how she'd manage if they brought her to the basement, though. Would the proximity be too close to block out? Perhaps the other girl would struggle just the same if they were both to be imprisoned in the same place. Had that girl lain below in the basement listening to screams from above? Lauren had screamed a lot.

Not anymore, though.

She wasn't Lauren anymore. She wasn't screaming anymore.
It wasn't like anyone would hear her anyway.
Out here in the mountains, no one could hear her scream.

1. LOST THIS TIME

The final hues of diminishing light were leeched from the sky by a ravenous dark. Stars appeared in their stead; pinpricks of ancient luminescence scattered above like raindrops on a celestial ocean. Megan's breath puffed out before her like tiny clouds. Trust her to get stuck with a rental car that had no heating.

"It's a bit banjaxed," the young man in the office had told her, his Irish accent thick and lyrical. "A good, hard rap of a fist should get it going again if it goes on the blink, love."

Megan had hit it "A good, hard rap" but so far, nothing. As daylight fell away to darkness and the cold began to seep into the vehicle, her foggy exhalations quickly accumulated into delicate cloud formations.

"What kind of idiot drives into the mountains in a strange country on their own?" she chided herself.

With one eye on the road and the other on the stereo, she twiddled the knob, desperately seeking something other than the hissing static that currently filled the void. The car continued to chug along the narrow, uneven road. Trees crowded in from either side, the moonlight whitewashing their branches to a dull shade, the colour of stripped bone. Every now and then, a low-hanging bough would knock against the roof of the car, each time causing her to jolt in her seat a little.

When she had first ventured into the Wicklow Mountains, the sun had still been high in the sky and the twitter of birds through the open windows had lent an air of cheer to her journey. Now, with nothing but radio static and darkness for company, Megan wasn't feeling quite so cheerful.

"You don't want to get stuck in the Vanishing Triangle on your own, especially after darkness falls," the car rental guy had told her.

"Vanishing Triangle?"

She knew immediately that he had regretted mentioning it, and from the short time she'd spent in Ireland so far, she was surprised when he hadn't continued talking. It wasn't the norm here from what she had experienced. The people here loved to talk, especially if it was a topic they themselves had broached in the first place.

Megan had landed in Dublin just over a week ago and spent her time since enjoying the sights and the locals. She'd never been anywhere with such open and friendly people. Complete strangers spoke to her as though they'd known her their whole lives. Back home in Boston that kind of friendly, outgoing nature was a rarity.

Dublin was such a small city, though, and the open road called to her.

The previous night, she had lain across the hard mattress in her budget hotel, ankles crossed, with a map of the island spread out before her. She'd Googled some of the place names that caught her eye and soon began to plot a course that would bring her on a tour of the country her father had called home.

Her dad had been very young when his family left for America, and he repeatedly told her a piece of his heart remained in Ireland. As a child, Megan had been horrified, picturing her dear old Dad reaching into his chest and pulling a piece of flesh from his still-beating heart before burying it in some secret location. As an adult, she knew what he meant, and now it gave her a feeling of wonderment, as though somewhere on this island she might stop off, knowing that *this* was the place he had meant. The invisible bonds that bound her heart to his, even now after death had stolen him from her, would somehow pull her subconsciously to the place where he had buried his heart, like a pirate burying his greatest treasure in the sands of some foreign shore.

And so, she had found herself at the nearest car rental office that was within her budget, the map neatly folded in her bag. Sure, she had her phone, but she wasn't idiot enough to think she'd get full coverage everywhere.

If you fail to plan, you plan to fail.

The old saying rattled around in her brain, something a teacher once told her, perhaps. "Was it Benjamin Franklin?" she'd mused, as she strode purposefully to the counter in search of a vehicle that would see her safely through her journey.

And here she was, driving around the mountains in what felt like circles in the middle of the night with no heat and no radio.

Well, based on the varying degrees of static, the radio was actually working; there just didn't seem to be any signal in these goddamn mountains.

With a sigh, Megan slowed down and scanned either side of the road for somewhere to pull in so she could check out the map, silently congratulating herself for planning ahead. Metal flashed in the car's headlights just ahead – a field gate – and she flicked the signal before cruising to a stop. Out here in the middle of nothingness, using her blinker seemed pointless, ridiculous even, but old habits (good habits, she reminded herself) die hard.

Reaching up to turn the interior light on, Megan groaned. Nothing. Nada.

"What else can go wrong with this fucking piece-of-shit car?!" she yelled, pummelling the steering wheel in frustration.

She rummaged in her bag, slid out her phone, and turned on the torch app. A quick glance at the display told her what she had already suspected: she had no signal on her phone out here in the sticks, so Google would not be assisting her. With a sigh, Megan unfolded the map and shone the torch across it. One thing she hadn't planned for was her inability to read a map.

It had seemed so easy and straightforward the night before, warm and safe inside her hotel room, excitedly marking a route. But now, looking at the squiggles and lines in front of her, she had no idea where she was. She hadn't consulted the map in hours, and definitely not since all the tiny little back roads and country lanes had started springing up everywhere like arteries.

Had she taken a wrong turn somewhere? Or missed a turn she should have taken?

Tears needled at the back of her eyes and Megan rubbed at them furiously with balled-up fists.

She wouldn't cry. Not yet.

Stuffing everything back into her bag, she flicked the signal again and pulled back out onto the road. She couldn't go in circles forever. Eventually she'd have to find a village or town, or even a house. Right?

The road continued in a gentle incline, gradually becoming steeper before levelling off again. The trees stood still like silent sentries on either side of the road, but every now and again black voids appeared, breaking up the shadowed darkness into inky black swathes. Megan wondered what kind of vista would lay before her if it were daylight and she could actually see through those breaks in the tree line. Her ears felt watery, and she pulled and stretched her mouth in a mimicry of yawning until she felt her ears pop. She had travelled higher than anticipated. It was so hard to tell in the pitch dark, the headlights of the rental car slicing through the blackness just enough to keep her safely on the road.

". . . know you'd never leave me behind, but I am lost."

The wheel jerked in Megan's hands as the radio suddenly came to life.

She allowed herself an ironic smile as she listened to the man's soulful voice. "You and me both, buddy!" She chuckled.

The music died away to static, and she reached across to turn the dial, hoping to find her new driving companion again. Just as his voice filled the car once more, *". . . in love and death we don't decide . . .",* a flash of colour beyond the windscreen caught Megan's attention. She looked up just in time to see a figure on the road, their bright yellow raincoat like a beacon in the night. With a scream, she pulled hard on the wheel. The car skidded along the gravelled surface and mounted the bank, coming to a grinding halt as it hit one of the sentinel trees.

Megan's face bounced off the steering wheel. *Guess the airbag doesn't work either,* she thought, as stars burst behind her eyes and pain flared in her face.

With an ominous crack, a huge bough separated from the tree and fell with a heavy crash onto the bonnet of the car. On the passenger side of the windscreen, the glass splintered but held.

Around her, everything fell silent but for the hiss and ticks of the battered engine.

There was a person on the road.

"Shitshitshitshit!" she cursed, red-hot pain flaring again as she turned to look at the space the yellow-clad figure had occupied just moments ago. Scanning the road and the ditches that ran alongside it for a body she hoped she wouldn't see, Megan sagged with relief as a blur of yellow dashed through the trees and away from her wrecked car.

"If they're moving, then they aren't dead," she whispered to herself, her eyes tracking the yellow coat until it was swallowed by the darkness. "If they're moving AWAY from me, then they're probably not a serial killer."

Probing her face gently, she winced, her fingers coming away sticky with blood. Panic bubbled up inside her, threatening to spill over as disorientation washed over her and her vision began to swim.

"Deep breaths. Deep breaths," she whispered to herself, dragging long, shuddering gulps into her aching lungs. Were they hurting because she was practically hyperventilating or because she'd broken something? A rib, maybe? Her lungs could be filling with fluid or blood, and here she was in the mountains, her car buried beneath a tree.

Panic ratcheted up within her, and before it could swamp her system entirely, she sucked in some more deep breaths – "cleansing breaths", her yoga instructor would have called them – until her heart rate slowly levelled out and the panic began to subside.

The surge of adrenaline that had flooded her veins was warring with the heavy fatigue that lay across her like a shroud, a feeling she recognised all too well from an adult life spent battling panic attacks. Well, at least since her dad had died.

She reached out and twisted the key in the ignition. It didn't seem likely that the car was going anywhere, buried beneath the ruins of the broken tree as it was, but the heater would certainly help if she was to be stuck here until first light. The engine didn't make a sound, not even a wheeze ushered from it. Not that it mattered, she realised, remembering that the heater on the stupid car hadn't worked anyway.

Reaching blindly behind herself, Megan pulled her coat and a blanket from the back seat of the car. The blanket had been one of her first purchases after landing, a fluffy green affair dotted with cute cartoon sheep. Back home, she had always slept with a fluffy throw, a holdover from childhood, but it hadn't been feasible to pack one for her trip to Ireland.

The perks of last-minute decisions made while trying to outrun the ones who hurt you.

Pulling the soft material across her trembling body, she was glad she'd bought it and that she'd left it within reach. As slim as her chances of finding a town or village had been before, they were zero now. Help wasn't coming anytime soon all the way out here. She could have a long walk ahead of her when the day's light finally returned to chase the darkness away.

Megan pulled the coat on top of the blanket and tugged her bobble hat further down over her ears. The lever for the seat still worked, so she reclined it and tried to get comfortable. Her breathing had relaxed, and she was pretty sure nothing was broken after all, except maybe her spirit, but that could always be rekindled.

She fell into a fitful sleep, her dreams plagued with familiar faces.

Her mother was there, as dismissive in her dream state as the woman was in real life.

"Meg," dream-Mom began, parroting the words she had said over the phone when Megan called her from Logan Airport, "Why must you always be so dramatic? Why can't you be more like Emily?"

In her dreams, Megan's half-sister Emily smirked from her place at their mother's side. Perfect Emily, the perfect product of her mother's perfect second marriage to rich douche, Eric. Ten years younger than Megan and somehow in their mother's eyes, infinitely more acceptable, Emily wasn't emotional or prone to "outbursts" like Megan. Emily was content to be a beige cardboard cut-out, perfect in every way and more than happy to do as her douche-dad wished. She didn't seem to have hopes and dreams of her own. All of Emily's ambitions were pre-approved by dear old Dad and his bottomless cheque book.

Megan had always tried to get along with her younger sister, but living such different lives left them worlds apart, even while they occupied each other's space.

"I'm not giving you money to squander, I'm afraid, Megan," chimed in Eric the Douche. He stood in her dream on the other side of her mother, disappointment – his default expression when dealing with Megan – evident on his suntanned face.

"I don't want your money, Eric," she responded, but the words fell from her mouth in a jumbled garble.

Dream-Eric raised an eyebrow.

Emily grasped at their mother's elbow, snickering behind her Barbie-pink nail polish.

Her mother just gazed at her with the same indifference as always.

Behind the trio, a shadowed figure clad in yellow moved closer. Megan tried to lean past her family to get a better look at the figure's face, but as is so often the case in the dreamworld, she couldn't make out any detail. Her family began to grow in size, blocking the figure out entirely. They started to laugh amongst each other, pointing their fingers at Megan, who had begun to shrink. The smaller she shrunk, the louder their laughter became, and although she cried and pleaded with them to stop treating her this way, they continued to. The laughter became cold and cruel, and suddenly, without warning, Emily lifted one dainty shoe and brought it down hard on Megan's tiny form.

With a jolt, Megan woke, panic clutching at her insides as the previous few hours raced through her mind, tangling with the dream that was already dissipating like smoke in the water. Outside, the darkness was still absolute, the moon hidden behind a heavy veil of cloud.

Colours sparkled in her vision, and she rubbed at her eyes, hoping it was just sleepy gunk and not a concussion from the crash affecting her vision. The colours were still there, and with a spark of excitement,

Megan realised they were coming from further away and slowly growing brighter as they moved closer. The lights of another vehicle!

Rubbing her sleeve on the foggy driver-side window, Megan screamed as a ghostly face peered back at her through the glass.

2. You're Safe With Me

Kicking against the door, she threw herself across the car as quickly as she could.

The figure's head turned; all detail lost within the hood of the yellow coat. The approaching vehicle was drawing closer, and the shadowy form beyond the door knocked at the window with a gloved hand, their hooded visage swivelling from the oncoming vehicle to Megan, and back again.

"Missus, open up. I can get you help," the hood said, its gruff voice distorted by the glass. "My house is just up the hill there. We've a phone you can use."

Whimpering, Megan tucked her body tighter against the passenger door, willing herself as far away from the stranger outside as possible. The voice came again, panic seeping through its tone.

"Open the door! They're almost here! I'm telling you now, missus, you're safer coming with me. You'd be an eejit to stay here."

Without warning, the stranger tugged at the handle, pulling frantically.

Offering up a silent prayer that she had had the foresight to lock the doors before she fell asleep, Megan strained to judge the distance of the oncoming vehicle. Her head whipped around, fresh pain flaring in her injured face, as she looked for something, anything, that she could use to defend herself should her would-be assailant gain entry into the car.

And then an idea burst forth, and Megan threw herself back across the seats. Her heart hammered in her chest, and she could hear the strained grunts of the figure as they continued to pull on the handle. She leaned on the horn, the sound cutting through the air outside like a siren.

The figure straightened, the hood falling back. Through the glass, their eyes met, and Megan gasped.

It was a man on the other side of the window, probably in his early fifties if she were to hazard a guess, but possibly younger. A jagged scar zigzagged along his face, silver and harsh looking by the light of the moon. A mop of curls lent an air of innocence to him and for a moment, Megan almost considered unlocking the door. Her gaze returned to the angry scar. His eyes hadn't seemed angry, though. They were soft and fearful. Her hand hovered by the mechanism, her eyes never leaving his, when lights blazed and a horn honked in answer to her own.

The other vehicle, close enough now for her to see that it was some kind of jeep, appeared to speed up, and when she turned her head back, the man was gone. Once more, she could see his silhouette as he wended his way through the trees and scurried up the hill, a ghostly yellow apparition in the darkness.

The jeep ground to a screeching halt right next to her car.

Megan peered through the glass as two figures emerged.

The driver, an older man with a gruff face, approached her car cautiously. He gazed at her impassively through the glass before knocking gently on the window.

"'Scuse me, are you okay? Any injuries?" he called.

Megan hesitated before unlocking and pushing the door open, her eyes never leaving the man's face.

"It's a girl," he called over his shoulder towards the other man whose features were hidden in shadow beneath the peak of a baseball cap. "Miss, are you okay? What happened?"

"I . . . I got lost. I'm not from around here," she whispered, her throat hoarse and dry.

The man looked at her.

"No shit," he replied. "I'd have never guessed with that accent. She's American, Finn. Or is it Canadian? Wouldn't be the first time I've mixed those up."

The other man, Finn, whistled and tossed something through the air. The older man caught it with barely a glance. He held the water bottle out and Megan took it gratefully. She chugged it down, the cold, clear liquid soothing her parched throat like a nectar sent straight from the heavens. Twisting the cap back on, she dragged a sleeve across her mouth and winced. Gingerly, she touched a finger to her lips. Her bottom lip hurt, and she could feel the puffiness from the swelling. Probably lucky that all her teeth were still intact after the smack she had taken from the steering wheel.

"Thank you," she said, smiling up at the man and proffering a hand. "I'm Megan."

He reached out, his gloved hand swallowing hers. "Seamus," he said. "But they all call me Shay. That's my boy, Finn." He jerked his head towards the tall figure just as they closed the rear door on the jeep.

The other man moved towards Megan, and as he passed through the headlights of the jeep, she could see what he carried and was struck by a fresh wave of panic. A long coil of rope hung from one shoulder, and in his hand was an axe.

"Jesus fucking Christ!" she whimpered, scurrying backwards into the car again, her eyes darting around like a wounded animal searching for an escape.

"Ah, calm the fuck down, will you?" Shay barked sharply, his head on a swivel, as though there was a crowd around to witness the scene she was making. He shook his head, embarrassed, muttering under his breath.

Megan watched through wide eyes as the other man strolled over casually, dropping the axe as he reached the driver-side door. It hit the road with a metallic clunk.

Dropping to his haunches, his eyes level with hers, Finn grinned. "Do you expect me to pull the fucking car out of the ditch with me bare hands, then?"

Blushing furiously, Megan was finally glad of the dark. It hid her embarrassment well.

She smiled shyly back, and his grin widened. She blushed again but for an altogether different reason.

The man before her was possibly the most handsome person she had ever seen. His skin had an olive tone to it, his face angled just right to showcase his dark eyes, silhouetted by long lashes. His bottom teeth were a little uneven but somehow, it only added to the overall effect. Dark hair peeked from beneath the cap on his head, and Megan found herself wondering what it was like without the hat covering it. What it might feel like beneath her fingers.

As though reading her thoughts, Finn winked at her before standing upright again. Still smiling cheerfully, he grabbed the axe and sauntered over to the tree that the rental car had hit. It was skewed slightly, more visibly angled than its poker-straight brethren. He hefted the axe, sizing up his target before swinging. It bit into the tree with a heavy thud.

Megan watched in fascination as he pulled up his sleeves, her eyes wandering to the flexing muscles of his forearms. Beside her, Shay coughed to gain her attention, and Megan thanked the night once more for disguising her flaming cheeks.

"This might take a while," he said. "Best if you aren't in the car, 'case something happens and the tree falls the wrong way."

He guided her towards the jeep, his hand hovering near her elbow but not quite touching it. She climbed inside their vehicle, glad of the heat that enveloped her.

Shay moved closer to her, his eyes never leaving hers. His face was weathered, but Megan guessed that he wasn't as old as he looked. Still old by her twenty-five-year-old standard, though. As he continued to move closer, her heart thumped heavily in her chest. *Is he going to try to kiss me?* she thought to herself, an awkward approximation of a smile frozen on her face. As he closed the distance between them, Megan continued to hold his gaze, and what she found there frightened her.

3. Potato, Potahto

His eyes were dead. Like the eyes of a shark or some other creature just as predatory.

Her pulse jumped at the base of her neck, and with horror, she watched as his eyes flicked down to her quivering throat and back up again. So quickly that it would have been practically imperceptible had she not been staring right at him. Time slowed down and it felt as though liquid ice had replaced the blood that flowed through her veins. Her skin crawled. He was so close now that she could see the small broken veins that dotted his cheeks and the pockmarks on his skin that were probably old scars from a long-forgotten skin condition. A scream slowly built inside her, and her mind tried to focus on the younger, beautiful man who stood just beyond the vehicle, whacking the tree with his axe.

And then, just as suddenly as it had begun, the strange moment had passed.

Shay continued moving past her, reaching down and rummaging around in a rucksack on the floor at her feet. Satisfied that he'd found what he was looking for, he straightened himself with a grunt, a flask held in his gloved hand.

"You must be starving," he said. "The missus never lets us leave without a flask of stew. We're rarely gone long enough to eat it, but it doesn't stop her from sending it. It'll warm your bones."

He twisted the cap and flipped it over to use as a cup. Steam wafted from the container as he poured, the fragrant scent of meat and herbs flowing from the rich, brown soup.

Megan swallowed, her stomach contracting hungrily.

For the second time in as many minutes, she gratefully accepted what Shay offered.

"Eat as much as you want," he said before closing the door.

Megan watched as his shadowed figure moved around the jeep and joined his son, still working hard to remove the tree.

The steam from the cup in her hands wafted upwards, the tantalising aroma making her mouth water. Blowing on the stew, she sipped cautiously. Her stomach rejoiced as it accepted the delicious offering. Tilting the cup, she swallowed greedily, the tender pieces of meat melting on her tongue. Not quite able to discern what type of meat she was ingesting, Megan shrugged and poured from the flask, filling the cup to the brim. This time, she ate slower, savouring all the flavours, along with the beautifully tender meat. She really hoped it wasn't something gross, like sheep or goat. Pushing images from her mind of cute little lambs with bells and ribbons around their necks and funny goat videos she had watched countless hours of on YouTube, Megan focused on the warm stew. She wished fleetingly for a thick, buttered slice to soak up the rich soup, her nostrils flaring as she imagined the scent of fresh baked soda bread.

Always an adventurous heart and eager to try the local wares, in her short time in Ireland, Megan had discovered a love for the traditional soda bread. The budget hotel she had spent her first few nights at offered it with every meal, and she had gratefully chewed and swallowed every morsel of it that she could get her hands on. Paired with the thick, salty butter that was also an Irish staple, it made for a filling and delicious snack. A nice, crusty slice would pair wonderfully with this stew.

Slurping down the remnants of her second helping, Megan screwed the top back on the flask and tucked it beside her on the seat.

Lulled by the rhythmic sound of the axe, coupled with the heat radiating from the warm flask and the fluffy sheep blanket she had pulled back around her, Megan soon nodded off.

With a jerk, she awakened, her mind a jumble of fragmented pieces unwinding the story of how she came to be asleep on the back seat of a strange vehicle with a smiling handsome man sitting across from her.

"Sorry if I woke you!" Finn called cheerfully. "Have the ropes tied on now, so I'm gonna try to free your car from the ditch."

"It's not my car. It's a rental," she replied dumbly, the haze of sleep still wrapped around her like a spider's web.

"Potato, potahto," Finn said with a smile before turning in his seat and firing up the engine.

The engine groaned, and Megan sat up straighter to watch through the tinted glass of the back seat window as the jeep crept forward. The rope uncoiled like a snake, straightened, and became taut. Shay stood watching, moving his hands in a way Megan could only assume made sense to Finn, whose head hung from the open window. Pulling the blanket a little tighter around her frame as cold fingers of night air crept along any exposed skin it could find, she watched through the back window as the men worked to free the car.

With a shudder, the rental car moved, slowly cutting a path through the sprinkling of fresh sawdust on the ground around it. Once it was clear of the ditch, Shay barked an order at Finn, who pulled up the handbrake and jumped from the jeep, the engine left idling.

Megan watched with curiosity as the pair circled the rental car, tightening ropes and double-checking things unseen from her vantage point. They stood close together for a moment, heads bowed towards each other in quiet conversation. Every now and again, one or the other would look over at the jeep. At her.

To her relief, Finn broke away from his father and returned to the jeep, opening the back door and climbing in beside her. He pulled a rectangular case from a pocket in the back of the driver's seat and opened it to reveal a small first aid kit.

"Got a little banged up," he said softly, as he cupped her chin gently and studied her face for damage. "Still beautiful, though."

Feeling flustered, warmth pooled throughout her body as she stared into his eyes. They were like bottomless pits. A deep stormy grey, like a tumultuous ocean. She caught herself just before she sighed dreamily, chiding herself for being such an idiot.

Hissing, she jerked back as he wiped her cuts and abrasions with alcohol wipes. With a gentle tut and a mischievous grin, he caught her face gently again and continued, his handsome face twisted in concentration.

After another few minutes of wiping and dabbing, he released her chin. "There ya go. Almost as good as new. Might take a few days for some of those cuts to heal, and there's gonna be bruises, but it'll all heal fine."

"Thank you," she whispered, not wanting to break eye contact. She felt like she could stay lost in his gaze forever. There was a weird sense of safety about him. "How often do you have to fix people up around here? You seem like a dab hand at it."

"I'm a vet by trade," Finn said with a smile as he stuffed everything back in the case and returned it to the seat pocket. "Isn't a huge difference between people and animals, except I prefer animals. Usually."

Her stomach twisted as butterflies fought to escape it, and Megan felt like groaning at her own ridiculousness. She wasn't normally such an easy target for flirty men, but something about this one just turned her insides to jelly. "Can you give me a ride into a town or somewhere that I can grab a phone?" she asked.

"I'll do one better! You can come home to ours. You must be wrecked after all that's happened. Ma always has the spare room ready for guests, so you can get some proper rest and get some food into you before dealing with everything. We're gonna tow the car now. It'll be grand and safe at our place, rather than being left on the roadside for anyone to vandalise it."

Megan smiled warmly at him.

"That sounds amazing. I appreciate it so much."

Finn opened the door and jumped out.

"Da will drive the jeep. I'll have to hop into your car to steer and whatnot, so I'll see you back at the house." There was a wistfulness in his voice as he spoke, and his gaze lingered on Megan for a moment before he shut the door.

Her heart sank knowing that it would be the gruff, older man driving with her, but a small pit of excitement also burned inside her. She had been instantly smitten with Finn, and she was pretty sure the feeling was mutual. This could turn out to be very interesting indeed. Megan wasn't usually one for believing in fate and destiny, but maybe the universe put her in that shoddy car and on this godforsaken mountain road in the dark for a reason. Maybe she was supposed to meet Finn.

As she ruminated on her circumstances, Shay slid into the driver's seat. He grunted something unintelligible back at her before starting the engine and taking off at a slow crawl, gradually building up some speed. His head swivelled back and forth from the rearview mirror to the one on the wing, keeping an eye on the progression of the car attached to the tow bar. He didn't say anything to Megan for the duration of the journey, and she happily disappeared into her own thoughts about Finn. She wondered if he was thinking about her too. Her time in Ireland was still young and plentiful. She could go for a little holiday romance with a tall, dark, and handsome stranger. Especially one with an Irish accent.

4. We're a Friendly Bunch

The jeep finally started to slow after what felt like an age but was, in reality, only about twenty minutes. In all the excitement, she hadn't thought to grab her handbag or her phone, so the time spent travelling passed in a meaningless vacuum. Shay hadn't spoken throughout the trip, but as the jeep slowed, he angled his head slightly and called over his shoulder, "Almost home now, my darling."

The casual use of terms of endearment in this country had grown on Megan quickly. It seemed to foster a feeling of closeness, one that her relationships back home were sorely lacking. One of the regular staff members during her stay in the hotel in Dublin repeatedly called her *sweetheart*, while a random elderly gentleman at a nearby corner store had called her *honey*. It made her giggle at the time, and the old man had beamed, delighting in her response.

Megan peered out the window with curiosity, still seeing nothing but huge swathes of forest interrupted by the occasional field.

The first beige rays of dawn were fighting to break through the night, but growing clouds, the colour of bruises, were winning in the struggle against the light. It looked as though a storm was building in the distance and building quickly. As though summoned by the very notice of the clouds, fat drops of rain began to fall, slowly at first, then gathering in pace and strength. The rain drummed against the roof of the jeep.

Through the driving rain and rolling rivulets that wended a hundred pathways along the glass, Megan watched as a laneway opened up among the trees. The jeep turned onto it, moving slowly to allow for the car being towed behind it.

The lane appeared to wind up the hillside forever, the trees arching across it like lovers straining to embrace one another. It darkened an already dull morning as they chugged slowly up through the trees. All of a sudden, the forest fell away, and a large patch of land opened up in front of them. Aside from the laneway entrance, the land was surrounded on all sides by deep, craggy cliffs of dirt, the tops of which were ringed by more trees. It looked as though some terrible force had cleaved right through the forest, leaving a bowl-like plot in its wake, like a blemish. An open sore amid the beauty of the untouched woodland that surrounded it.

In the middle of the plot sat a house, surrounded closely by a handful of structures – most small but one large enough in itself to be another house. A big rolling metal door stood open, a shape moving around inside in the weak light. *Must be a garage*, Megan thought to herself, recognising the shadowed outlines of vehicles within.

She studied the house as they approached it. It was a huge, sprawling structure with peeling paint and a veritable jungle growing along the gutters, plant life reaching up towards the dark tiled roof as if seeking to cover it entirely. The windows all stood dark and silent, but as they drove closer, a light flicked on in the lower half. Someone had been awaiting their arrival.

Finn and Shay's arrival, she reminded herself.

In that instant she became acutely aware that she was about to impose on a family of complete strangers in some remote mountain home in a strange country. This felt like the start of every horror movie she had ever watched. Then Finn's stormy eyes flashed in her mind, and the fist of dread in her stomach dissipated as it burst into a thousand fluttering butterflies once more.

The jeep pulled around the front yard in a wide arc, Shay checking his mirrors again until he was satisfied with the rental car's proximity to the garage. The engine died, and the atmosphere became thick and awkward as the two sat in silence.

"Thank you for coming to my rescue," Megan said, eager to break the strange tension that was almost suffocating.

Turning in his seat, Shay stared at her, his face void of expression. A noise rumbled from his throat, and as it carried into the space around them, Megan realised he was chuckling to himself. Still, he sat, that expressionless gaze holding hers. Then, like the sun breaking from behind storm clouds, his face lit up and he smiled at her.

He waved a hand as he turned back in his seat. "G'way out of that. Sure, we couldn't leave you sitting in the dark by yourself now, could we? Me and the boys will sort your car out, get it in out of the weather and whatnot for the time being. You can head on into the house and warm up."

Megan's heart galloped in her chest.

"Just walk inside. But it's not my house. That seems rude."

Shay threw his head back and laughed.

"Jaysus, you haven't been in Ireland long, have you? We're a friendly bunch. No such thing as knocking for entry around these parts, darling." He turned towards her again, laughing when he saw her panic-stricken face. "If it makes you feel any better, our Finn has already gone in ahead of you. He'll have the aul one filled in before you even make it to the front door."

She turned her head to look, and sure enough, the rental car was empty. Finn was nowhere to be seen. As if in answer, more lights came on in the downstairs windows, and an outside light flickered to life from the porch.

"Told you!" Shay said, still chuckling as he hauled himself from the jeep. Without another word, he ambled the short distance to the garage and disappeared into its gloom.

With a deep breath to steel her nerves, Megan pushed the blanket off her, instantly missing its warmth and wishing she could take it with her. She supposed she could, but it was nerve-wracking enough to walk into a stranger's house without doing it wrapped in a fluffy blanket with cartoon sheep on it. Even the thought of that made her cringe.

She hopped from the jeep, the cold sting of rain instantly washing the nervousness from her bones, and hustled towards the house. The air smelled like wet leaves and damp earth, with an unmistakable undertone of a farmyard mixture of animals and shit. Hopping up the few steps that led to the porch, she was instantly glad that the entranceway was covered. She was still cold, but at least the rain couldn't reach her. Hesitating at the threshold, Megan jumped as the door swung inwards.

A small woman stood peering out at her, her mouth set in a grim line.

Megan's stomach dropped.

"You must be Megan! Come on, come inside. You'll freeze out there. Weather's taken an awful turn!"

The woman pulled Megan through the door and deeper into the house.

5. THE GEORGIE DENBROUGH OF THE WICKLOW HILLS

"God, you've really had an awful few hours, love, haven't you?" the woman said, sliding a loaded plate onto the table in front of Megan.

She nodded and inhaled deeply, her hungry eyes roving over the food. Meat patties, freshly fried and tossed onto thick crusty bread with dollops of butter melting along the sides, and a generous helping of golden fried potatoes. The scent of fried food hung in the air around the gloomy kitchen, a much nicer smell than the slightly musty odour that seemed to permeate the place when she first arrived. Megan had just recounted her time in Ireland at the woman's behest, and now she picked up one of the sandwiches and took a glorious bite, savouring the flavours on her tongue.

"I think this is one of the nicest things I've tasted since I arrived in Ireland," Megan complimented through a mouthful of food.

"Freshest meat you'll get," the older woman said. "We keep our own pigs out back. The difference in taste is astonishing." She sat down across from Megan, tea sloshing over the rim of her cup as she placed it on the scuffed wooden table. Leaning back in her chair, she appeared to study the younger woman, her intelligent eyes probing.

Megan couldn't figure the woman out. When she had first ushered her into the house, she had been friendly, but every now and again as she bustled around the kitchen preparing food, Megan caught her occasional ambivalent glances. A long silence became filled with chatter and probing questions again very suddenly, and it gave Megan mental whiplash. The woman's accent was more British than Irish, which took Megan by surprise, but she had clearly lived here a long time. Her mannerisms and speech were very similar to what Megan had encountered in the country so far. Her appearance was the biggest surprise of all. In the darkened entryway, she'd looked almost exactly like Megan had imagined a spouse of someone like Shay to look: small and unassuming, elderly, made even older by years of mountain living. Beneath the brighter lights in the kitchen, though, she'd appeared almost youthful. She had a stiff walk and the strained look of someone with years of hard work behind them – a dried-up, exhausted kind of aura, but beneath the lined skin, there was something else. A kind of vitality that hadn't been shaved away by time or harsh mountain air. Her hair was pulled back from her face in a tight ponytail of dark roots that bled into a dirty yellow-blonde colour. Most likely the result of a bad bottle dye job. Megan had seen the results of so many unfortunate home dye attempts in high school that it turned her off colouring her own hair, which hung to her shoulder in chestnut strands.

The woman looked as though she could be anywhere between fifty and eighty years of age.

Licking butter from her finger, Megan plucked a golden potato wedge from the plate and smiled across the table at the woman, who still studied her. "Thank you so much for the meal. You've all been so accommodating; I don't know how I'll ever repay you."

The woman continued to hold her gaze.

"You'll find a way. The universe will see to it," the woman said, finally breaking her gaze to pick up the steaming mug.

"I don't think I caught your name," Megan said apologetically.

"I didn't tell you it. You can call me Ma," she said with a tight smile. "That's what everyone else does. Ma, Ma, Ma, that's all I hear. Sometimes I think I live with a flock of sheep instead of a house full of men."

She chuckled, and Megan giggled along with her.

"So it's all boys, then?" Megan asked.

Ma looked towards the far wall wistfully. It was littered with photo frames in all shapes and sizes, most under a thin coating of dust. "Not always," she said, her voice almost a whisper. "I had a little girl once. Matilda."

She looked away from the pictures, and Megan's own eyes fell down towards her plate. It didn't feel right to continue staring at the pictures while the old woman was clearly hurting. She took another sip from her cup before continuing.

"Tilly was the most beautiful child I had ever seen. I know you probably think I'm biased as her mother, but my Tilly was an angel."

"Was?" Megan whispered, her hands itching to reach across the table to Ma, whose eyes were glittering with unshed tears.

"I'd rather not talk about it, if you don't mind, darling. I'll make fresh tea. Will you have some?"

With a nod, Megan stood and carried her empty plate to the sink. A quick scan showed no obvious dishwasher, so she grabbed the dishcloth and turned on the faucet. As she scrubbed the plate under the steaming water, she felt Ma's eyes burning into her back. *Was she about to chastise her for being too familiar?* Megan knew the Irish appreciated, even welcomed, familiarity. Perhaps she judged wrong with this woman, though. According to her accent, after all, she *wasn't* actually Irish herself.

Placing the clean plate in the drying rack, Megan turned, but Ma faced away from her, back hunched over. Confused, Megan sat back down. Ma shuffled awkwardly to the table and sat, too, gently pushing one of the two steaming mugs across the table. Just as Megan was about to ask about her accent, Ma spoke up, "So, if you don't mind me asking, how did you come to be in a ditch, Megan? I don't think you mentioned it, and Finn never said."

At the mention of his name, Megan felt a blush crawl up her neck. Across from her, Ma straightened slightly.

"There was a person on the road."

"A person?" gasped Ma, her hand fluttering to her chest. "Are they okay?"

"Oh, I didn't hit them. That's how I ended up in the ditch. From swerving to avoid them," she said with a wry smile. "They ran off, then came back. Right before your husband and Finn came to my rescue, he was trying to force his way into my car."

Ma reached across the table and grasped Megan's hand gently. "Oh, my poor dear, that must have been quite scary! I'm so sorry you went through that. I swear, these mountains are generally quite safe."

"In hindsight, I don't think he meant me harm. I saw his face just before he took off. He had a bright yellow coat on, but the hood fell back. There was a huge scar on his face. He kept shouting that he could save me. It was pretty weird."

Just then, a door opened in the hallway.

Ma squeezed her hand. "A yellow coat, you say?"

"Yes," Megan said distractedly, her head cocking at the sound of shuffling boots and muffled laughter floating in from the direction of the front door.

Releasing her hand, Ma sat back against her chair, a hard smile on her face.

"Shay!" she called.

He responded with a grunt before appearing in the kitchen doorway, what little hair he had plastered to his head from the rain. Another man appeared behind him, and Megan's heart sank a little to see he was a stranger to her. Obviously, another son based on the resemblance to Shay. Whereas she pegged Finn to be much closer in age to herself, if a little older perhaps, the man before her now was probably closer to forty. He had the ruddy complexion and auburn hair of his father. His face, although smiling, appeared twisted in a sneer, and he had the same soulless eyes as Shay.

Both men trod into the room, Shay taking what was presumably his designated seat at the head of the table. The younger man propped himself against the kitchen counter where the worktop met in a *V* shape.

"Flick the kettle, please, Ollie," Ma said, not even turning to look at her son. "Shay, you'll never guess who was trying to get to our girl here!"

Shay looked from Ma to Megan, the confusion clear on his face. "What are you on about, woman?" he grumbled.

"Liam O'Keefe. He was standing in the road in that yellow raincoat. That's why Megan had to swerve into the ditch in the first place! And the bollox came back and tried to get into the car after her – to save her!" Ma grew more animated with each word she spoke.

"Fucking Liam," muttered Shay.

"Yeah, fuckin' Liam," the other man – Ollie – echoed from the corner.

"What about Liam?"

Megan's heart soared as Finn stuck his head through the door, headed to the sink, then began wringing the soaking baseball cap in his hands. He beamed at her and strode across to his brother at the kettle, slicking his dark hair back with one hand as he went.

"Liam O'Keefe was the one that caused the American to crash her car," his dad replied. "Was trying to save her just before we showed up but terrified the girl by all accounts. No wonder you were so jumpy when we found you."

This last aside was directed at Megan, though he didn't look at her as he spoke.

Finn barked a laugh. "Are you serious?"

"In his fuckin' yellow raincoat," Ollie said, nudging his brother in the ribs.

"That fuckin' yellow coat," Finn said, shaking his head, his mouth split in a grin. "He's like the Georgie Denbrough of the Wicklow hills."

The sneer faded from Ollie's face. "Who's Georgie Denbrough?"

Finn sighed and rolled his eyes.

"Pick up a fucking book every now and again, Ollie. It'll expand your mind. Although if it expands much more, that one fuckin' brain cell of yours might roll right out of you."

Shay howled with laughter.

Ollie narrowed his eyes at Finn, who stuck his tongue out at his brother before pulling out the wooden chair next to his mother and slouching into it. Glancing across at him, Megan could see no resemblance between Finn and the rest of his family. Ollie looked to be an almost carbon copy of his father. Ma was the polar opposite of them all. Small framed and frail looking, she seemed dwarfed by the men that surrounded her. Against the coppery-yellow bottle blonde colour, those dull brown roots interwoven with strands of steely grey seemed almost luminous beneath the kitchen fluorescents.

Finn met Megan's eyes across the table and winked. Her face flamed once more, and she cursed herself and her stupid schoolgirl crush. He sure was pretty, though!

Ollie placed steaming mugs in front of his father and brother before seating himself and sipping from his own. Proper introductions were made between Megan and Ollie, and the small group chatted idly about the inclement weather outside. The start of a potential storm, Ma said, according to the local radio station.

"Well, I'd better get out there and check on the hogs before the weather gets any worse," Finn said as he stood and stretched. His jumper rode up and Megan gulped as she caught a brief flash of taut, tanned skin.

"Throw a few extra blankets into the guest room from the hot press when you're passing, please, Finn," Ma called after his retreating form. Her eyes moved to Megan. "You need to get some rest soon. You've been through a stressful few hours, but some proper sleep will fix you up better than anything."

Megan smiled gratefully at the older woman, who soon dropped her gaze and sat quietly as her husband and son discussed a trip to gather supplies before the storm became too fierce. Megan tried to interject and involve herself in their conversation, but they had ceased to notice her presence. She tried to catch Ma's eye and start a conversation, perhaps ask some more questions about her accent and what had brought her to Ireland, but the older woman's gaze remained steadfastly on a deep gouge in the worn wooden table, her withered fingers following the path it carved along the surface. Unsure if it was her imagination or not, Megan felt stifled by a subtly building atmosphere in the cramped room. But before the lull in conversation could become unbearably awkward, a bloodcurdling scream pierced the silence.

6. More Tea?

The scream floated up through the scuffed linoleum floor as though the very foundations of the house were shrieking in torment.

Eyes wide, Megan jumped as heavy rock music burst forth in its wake. Her panicked gaze swung to Ma, who averted her eyes, picking up her cup and sipping from it. Her face wrinkled in disgust and a drizzle of tea leaked from her mouth and back into the now cold cup.

Looking to Shay, Megan opened her mouth to speak, her hands trembling in her lap, but he cut her off before the words could come tumbling from her frozen throat.

"Fucking Denis," he said, voice raised to be heard over the music. "How many times have I told that lad to keep that shite down?!" He chuckled then, shaking his head.

Megan looked from Shay to Ma, who still studied her tepid teacup, and back again.

"B... But... That was a scream. A woman just screamed!"

She pushed back from the table, preparing to escape. To where, she didn't know. Her fight-or-flight instinct had just kicked in, and it had clearly made its choice. If only her mother could see her now, running away from a problem once more! That howl of anguish was playing on a loop in her head, despite the crashing music that now bled through the floor.

Shay reached towards her, and she flinched. Seeing the panic in her eyes, he held his hands up in a gesture of innocence.

"My son, Denis. His room is in the basement. He forgets sometimes that being under the house doesn't mean we can't hear him. He's like a cave dweller. Practically a fuckin' Morlock down there. Spends far too much of his time tucked away listening to that infernal racket and watching the scary films. It's probably not polite to say to a stranger, but I'm at my wits' end with him. He's a pain in the arse. But he is harmless, and he's great with his hands. Our Denny can work wonders and shite miracles with a combustion engine."

"What's a Morlock, Da?"

Shay rolled his eyes at Ollie and offered Megan a conspiratorial wink. "Finn's right, Ollie. Pick up a fucking book!"

Despite herself, Megan giggled into her hand and relaxed a little in her chair, accepting his explanation.

A basement. Another son. Just how many kids did this man have?

She offered a small smile, and in return Shay reached forward and patted her hand gently.

"Ollie, run down and have a word with Denny, please. Tell him we have company. Tell him dear old Da said to cop onto himself."

Ollie stood and dutifully left the room. A door opened a short distance away, its hinges creaking before banging shut again. Not too long after, the music cut off abruptly.

"Much better," Shay said with a sigh of satisfaction. "More tea?"

HUSH, MY DARLING

It hadn't taken long for the multiple cups of tea to travel straight to her bladder, and Megan asked for directions to the bathroom and excused herself.

The hallway, like the small portion of the house she had seen so far, was dark and dreary, the dull light that bled from the lightshades not helped by the darkening day outside. Moving along the narrow hall, Megan noticed a distinct lack of family photos out here. There was plenty of generic artwork adorning the walls, a mishmash of painted landscapes, floral arrangements, and oddly grotesque paintings of naked people and religious tableaus, but no photographs. After witnessing the huge display on the back wall of the kitchen, she was surprised that the theme didn't carry through the house.

Spying the bathroom, Megan slipped inside and locked the door, relieved to finally have a few moments to herself.

7. Take Her On a Date First

Her bladder now empty and feeling much more comfortable, Megan stood at the discoloured sink pedestal. She tried to study her reflection in the small mirror that hung askew on the wall, but the glass was smoky with age and splintered with cracks. With a sigh, she leaned down and splashed her face with water from the tap, hissing as the cold liquid reminded her of the damage to her face. Outside the door, a board creaked.

Straightening quickly, she eyed the door cautiously.

"Hello?"

Only silence greeted her.

Turning back to the basin, she shut off the water and dried her hands on a surprisingly clean towel, a soft green one embroidered with small lilac flowers on the edges. She smiled to herself, enjoying the odd find of something so obviously feminine hiding in plain sight in such a masculine environment. Ma must be one tough lady, indeed, to survive here among all these boys!

Still smiling, Megan pulled the bathroom door open.

And screamed.

A face loomed at her, big and round like a pudgy moon. It creased into an approximation of a smile, crooked yellowing teeth jutting from its gums like mossy old gravestones in a cemetery. It reached a gnarled hand out and stroked her face, its fingers trailing along her jaw, lower, tracing the outline of her clavicle and swooping along the curve of her breast. Megan shuddered and shrieked in disgust, and just as suddenly as it had appeared, the figure was yanked away from her.

"Jesus, Grandad! Take her on a date first!"

Megan peered around the corner at the snickering face of an adolescent boy, probably about fifteen or sixteen. His face was streaked with the teenage curse of acne, but his frame was lean and without the puppy fat that afflicted most young boys.

He saluted her before whipping around and leading the old man down the hallway. They disappeared into the shadows as Shay appeared in the doorway, Ma shuffling along behind him in that staggered, limping fashion she had.

"You met my aul da, then?" Shay chuckled.

Megan stared at him, her face set in a rictus of horror.

"He meant you no harm," came a voice from behind her.

She spun around, facing the teenager again.

"He's riddled with dementia. Hasn't a clue if he's coming or going. Honestly, missus, he rarely gets out of his bed, let alone leaves his room."

Megan looked from the boy's grinning face to Shay's. She cast her eyes towards Ma, but the woman turned her head, looking everywhere but at her.

"He assaulted me! He touched my . . . my . . . me."

Shay patted her arm, his face struggling to hold back the mirth that threatened to spill over. "Apologies, Megan. You'll probably never see him again, if that makes you feel any better. We can lock his door while you're still around."

She gaped at him, horrified once more.

"Well, there's hardly any need to lock him in. I mean . . . he's an old man. That seems cruel. It's fine, I just got a fright, is all."

With a warm smile, Shay linked her arm. "This is another of the Brogan clan," he said, gesturing towards the boy. "This is my grandson, Michael. He belongs to Denny. You haven't met him yet, but he's the one down below in the basement. Gets harder and harder to keep track of all these boys!"

He slapped young Michael on the shoulder heartily.

Michael smiled and waved at Megan. He was smaller than the rest of the men and had the same piercing blue eyes as Ma.

Finally, someone who didn't resemble Shay.

Although it still left Finn as a mystery. He was like an exotic flower among dandelions and weeds, with his golden complexion and smouldering darkness. Megan shook herself from her reverie and wiggled her fingers in a return greeting, offering the boy a half-hearted smile. He moved along the hallway, stopping briefly to give Ma a quick hug as he passed her.

Megan melted a little, instantly warming towards the boy who clearly loved his grandma.

"You ready to catch some rest?" asked Ma, her features softened from the embrace she had shared with her grandson.

With a nod, Megan followed the woman as she shuffled down the hallway.

They moved deeper into the house, Megan glancing occasionally at the impersonal art that dotted the faded wallpaper. It was a continuation of the pictures that had hung between the kitchen and the bathroom. The house looked as though it stretched on forever, much further than the exterior had suggested, and she found herself idly wondering if the basement also stretched the same distance. What kind of cavernous space must they have down there? Did they need it to house all the men and boys who seemed to materialise so very frequently?

Brogan.

She realised that Shay's introduction of Michael in the hallway had been the first time she had heard their surname. It seemed suitably Irish and conjured images of the *brogue* shoes worn by the traditional Irish dancers she had watched in a pub in Temple Bar on one of her first nights out in Dublin, and of the lilting Irish *brogue*, the lyrical accent that varied from one person to the next. An image came to her unbidden: the curly-haired man in the rental car office.

You don't want to get stuck in the Vanishing Triangle on your own . . .

"What's the Vanishing Triangle?" she asked suddenly, the words tumbling from her mouth before she could stop them.

In front of her, Ma froze before spinning slowly on her heels.

"Vanishing Triangle?" Ma asked coolly.

"Yeah. The guy in the car rental place mentioned it. He didn't elaborate, but it sounded creepy, the way he said it . . ." Her voice faltered as she trailed off awkwardly. She felt stupid for even mentioning it.

Ma looked at her for a moment before barking a laugh.

"Darling, I think that man was trying to trick you into some tourist trap type thing. Vanishing Triangle." She snorted and shook her head, turning back down the corridor.

A moment later, Ma stopped in front of a door.

It had once been wooden but had been painted white at some juncture, the colour peeling away in curls like orange rind. Turning the key, Ma swung the door inward with a flourish. "It's not a luxury hotel, but it's clean and cosy," she said quietly, her eyes downcast.

Megan stepped into the room, her eyes scanning its dull interior.

The carpet was worn, almost threadbare in places. Huge flowers swirled into each other, a palette of browns and creams that set the tone for the rest of the room. As her eyes travelled up the walls, she winced as she noticed the peeling edges of the wallpaper – also brown and cream – that reached up to a popcorn ceiling which very well could have once been white but was now a dull shade of nicotine yellow. Either someone had smoked in this room for years on end, or the ceiling just wanted to blend in with the rest of the drab décor. Save for the bed that extended from beneath one half of the large window, the only piece of furniture in the room was a dark wooden dresser that stood against the wall. It looked old, the brass handles on its drawers dull with age. A lamp sat atop it.

She continued scanning, her eyes falling on the curtains that were thankfully not brown but were still a rather startling shade of mustard yellow. The thick drapes were still pulled across the window as though someone had gone to bed here one night and disappeared into thin air, never to return and pull back the drapes to greet the morning sun.

"May I?" Megan asked, pointing to the drapes as she glanced at Ma.

"Go right ahead, though you're best off closing them again once you've had a look. Easier to rest in a darkened space."

Feeling a little embarrassed and more than a little chastised, Megan pulled the curtains apart.

The room was situated right at the back of the house, and small sheds and outhouse buildings dotted the immediate edge of the land. The space stretched way back, small enclosures nestled together like a miniature village, presumably where the pigs were housed, she thought. In the far corner of the huge stretch of the yard stood a barn, its peeling red paint faded to a rusty orange. Behind the structure, the forest soared.

Dense thickets of trees reached for the darkened skies, surrounding the whole property like razor wire around a prison. Megan shuddered at the analogy, and she questioned her own morbid imagination. Movement caught her eye by one of the animal enclosures and she watched as two figures emerged from a shed and into the pouring rain. A third figure joined them from another enclosure. One of the men turned suddenly and raised an arm in greeting. *Finn*. Blushing, Megan turned back around to face Ma, but the doorway stood empty.

With a shrug, she closed the curtains and moved towards the bed. It was only large enough to accommodate one person, the iron frame lifting in an arch at its head and twisting in intricate curls. Lifting the blanket, she surveyed the sheets with a suspicious eye, but they looked clean. On the foot of the bed, two more large blankets were folded neatly – one brown, just like everything else in the room, and one pink, its edges laced with ribbon. *Another feminine touch in this oversized man cave*, she thought to herself with a chuckle.

Stepping lightly across the room, Megan closed the door. Remembering the key on the outside, she quickly pulled it open again, but the keyhole was empty. Her eyes scanned the hallway floor outside, but there was nothing there. Perhaps Ma had slipped it into her apron pocket, lest the younger boy Michael try to prank their guest. Who knew what kind of rambunctious mischief young boys got themselves into?

Closing the door softly once more, she made her way back across the room, the bone-weary tiredness finally beginning to weigh on her as she approached the bed. It looked so soft and inviting.

Stripping off her clothes, Megan slipped beneath the blanket, leaning forward to tug the extra blankets further up the bed to cover her cold and aching body. As her head hit the pillow, she felt the tension melt from her muscles, and with a sigh, she snuggled tighter under the covers.

She was asleep within seconds.

8. Hello There, Ted.

"I'll take you to Ireland someday, Megatron. That's our real home."

Megan squinted at her dad before throwing her head back and laughing. Her brown hair rippled as her shoulders shook. Her dad had never outgrown that stupid nickname. Didn't care if he embarrassed her in front of friends or boyfriends. But she didn't care either, and it never really did embarrass her. There was too much love and warmth in that stupid nickname to make her feel anything other than safe.

"What will we do first when we get there?" she had asked him.

"We'll go find my heart, of course, my love," he'd said, his gaze tender. "It belongs to you more than anyone. We might leave a little piece there, though, for old times' sake."

An ache pierced her heart as memories flooded in.

Dad, strong and safe, sitting her down to relay the bad news from the hospital tests. Dad, slowly withering before her eyes. Dad, accepting the medications, the spoon feeds, the bed baths, all of it with a quiet stoicism despite the way she knew it made his heart hurt and his pride ache. Not for himself, no. For her. Megan. His only daughter, only child. She was his everything, and never in a million years would he have wanted her to see him like that.

When her mom had left all those years ago to shack up with her douche-boss, Eric, it was just Megan and her dad. And things had been perfect. She wanted for nothing, and Dad had made every day an adventure as she grew from a curious, clever child to a smart young woman. He had made sure that she always looked at the world with curiosity and at the things within it with kindness.

And then she had come home that afternoon from work. The house was no different, but the atmosphere had changed. Megan always felt that she had known the second she opened the door. Dad lay in his bed, his face peaceful for the first time in months, a handwritten note, the words scrawled in looping cursive, clutched in his cooling hands. Empty pill bottles lay scattered across the bed's surface.

The following hours, days, weeks had passed in a confusing blur. Megan would always remember clearly the short time that passed between her finding her dad's body and calling the paramedics, though. She had sat and held his hand. Whispered to him all the things he had done right, all the ways he'd made her the person she was, and how much she would miss him. She forgave him for giving up because she knew that if she were in his position, she probably would have done the same thing. It wasn't selfishness that had driven him to take his own life. It was selflessness. Love for his daughter.

That same love shone in his eyes now, lighting them up from within, and Megan swallowed hard to dislodge the lump in her throat. She squeezed her eyes shut, a vain attempt at a barrier for the tears that fell unbidden.

Dad was dead. He wasn't really here. She had to be dreaming.

She felt his hand on her arm, his skin cold as she knew it should be.

"Open the door."

Megan's eyes flew open. Now, in her dad's place, sat the figure in the yellow raincoat.

"Open the door! You're safer with me." His voice rose an octave, his grip becoming tighter on her arm. It no longer felt safe. She tried to pull her arm back, and in response, the figure lunged towards her, his voice rising and twisting into a monstrous tone that made her hair stand on end.

"OpenupOpenupOPENUP," the figure roared, and as they moved closer, the yellow hood flopped backwards. Finn stared at her, his face almost touching hers, his dark eyes flashing and dangerous. His mouth opened wider and wider, cracks appearing on his golden skin, and even when his roars cut to silence, his mouth continued to stretch.

A new sound flowed from within, a delicate whimper that seemed entirely at odds with the stretching void of his mouth. A scratching started up, drowning out the sound of soft crying. It was as though the very teeth in his head were screaming, pulling themselves up by the roots to vacate this wide-open hellscape. Louder and louder the scratching grew, and Megan panted as the panic rose up her gorge and threatened to engulf her . . .

With a breathless yelp, she bolted upright. Her hands flew to her face, wiping away the remaining strands of her strange dream, like threads of a spider's web. The darkness was oppressive, thick as syrup around her. Panic had followed her from her dream, and she struggled to remember where she was and why she was encased in blackness.

And then it all came flooding back: the mountains, the accident, the Brogan family. Pressing a hand to her chest, Megan could feel her heart fluttering beneath her skin. As the room slowly came into focus, so, too, did her heartbeat slow.

Within the black now, she could see the outline of the dresser and the window. Reaching for her phone, she remembered that it was still in the car. With no torch to guide her, she slid from the bed and moved to the window. Pulling the heavy drapes aside, Megan was shocked to see the moon struggling to break through the clouds.

Nighttime! She had slept all day.

Rain fell in sheets and the surrounding forest rattled and shook in the wind. Behind her, the soft whimpering started again, the sound travelling through the darkness and curling around her like a freezing fog. Megan gasped, whirling around. She half expected to meet some kind of apparition head-on, so ghostly was the sound.

But she was still alone in the room. At least as far as she could see.

Megan moved towards the dresser. She remembered seeing the lamp on top, and after a quick wave of her hands around its vicinity, she found it and clicked it on. The small room flooded with a soft golden glow, and she squinted her eyes until they adjusted to the reintroduction of light.

Megan sat heavily on the bed. She had no way to tell the time and couldn't even begin to guess at it. The only sound was the storm outside as it raged through the mountains. Even the quiet crying had stopped.

And then, slowly, a scratching. A low scrabbling that grew louder as it approached the bedroom door. The dream came flooding back to her, and every muscle in Megan's body pulled taut in frightened anticipation. Her eyes didn't leave the door as the sound continued to grow.

And then, a heavy scratching right at the door, as though something was trying to burrow right through the old wood.

Before she could open her mouth to scream, the door burst open. She yelped in surprise as a brown blur flew towards her, pushed itself against her, wet nose sniffing at her. Its tongue slurped at anything it could reach.

It sat back and looked at her, its tail still a blur as it wagged side to side.

Megan regarded the dog.

It looked like it was smiling, its tongue lolling from its curved mouth. Sliding from the bed to the carpet, Megan reached out a hand. The dog barrelled forward again, panting as it rolled its body against her. Scratching its ears, she felt a smile creep upon her lips. How could she not smile? The creature was desperate to receive attention and just as desperate to give it.

It was a Labrador.

Its coat was rich and brown, a deep chocolate colour. As the animal squirmed and rolled in excitement, she got a glimpse beneath it and knew instantly that it was a male. She continued to stroke its ears, and satisfied that this human wasn't about to quit providing the attention it sought, the dog settled into her lap and promptly closed its eyes.

With another smile, she moved one hand down to the collar around the dog's neck and grasped the tag.

Ted.

"Well, hello there, Ted." She ran her fingers through his silky fur, ignoring the wet dog stink that wafted from him. He was warm and he was friendly, and that was all she needed right now. Moving the dog from her lap, Megan crawled back onto the bed and beneath the covers, then patted the surface. Ted jumped onto the bed and settled almost immediately, his snout resting on her covered chest. She stroked his head. The dog gazed at her through soulful golden eyes, and she watched in satisfaction as his lids slowly dropped and then closed completely. Her own followed soon after.

9. GOOD LUCK WITH THE SHEEP

If the gentle knocking on the bedroom door had not woken Megan, the sudden shifting of the dog on the mattress immediately after would have done the job. She opened her eyes, blinking the veil of sleep away, and caught the tail end of Ted as he leapt from the bed and crashed towards the door, his brown tail a blur of motion.

"Morning, sleepyhead."

Finn stood in the doorway, leaning casually against the wooden frame. As the dog approached, he dropped to his haunches, pulling Ted close and scratching the animal's ears enthusiastically. Pulling herself up on her elbows, Megan smiled shyly at him.

"What time is it?" she asked. "I woke up before, but it was full dark. I can't believe I slept for so long!"

Finn laughed, still stroking a jubilant Ted. "I did check in on you yesterday evening, but you were dead to the world. You had an eventful morning; I thought you deserved the rest. Although, I'm surprised you managed to sleep through that storm. If we had woken up to find the house had been lifted away to Oz, I honestly wouldn't have been surprised."

Megan laughed, then turned to the window.

Through a gap in the heavy drapes, a golden shaft of light had found its way inside. Dust motes danced within, swirling into a frenzied tornado as Ted left Finn's side to cross back to the bed. He jumped up and nestled back into the crook of Megan's legs, his muzzle resting on her thigh. She reached out and ran her fingers along his soft fur. His eyes closed in response.

"Seems you have a fan around here," said Finn, his eyes softening as he watched the dog.

"He frightened the life out of me last night. I was all caught up after a bad dream. At first, I thought I could hear crying. Then this guy started scratching at the door. I was just about ready to jump out of my skin when he barrelled in here. He made for great company, though."

Finn frowned. "Crying?"

With an awkward smile, Megan shrugged her shoulders. "It was my imagination. Unfamiliar house and all that. So, the storm has passed?"

Finn crossed to the window and grasped at the curtains, tilting his head towards her questioningly.

"Go ahead," she said with a wave of her hand.

He pulled the drapes apart and sunlight flooded the room.

"I'd love to tell you yeah, but it's only a little reprieve. Ma says the weatherman said it'll be back with a vengeance later tonight. Good news, though! Da and Denny have started fixing up that car of yours. I brought your handbag in for you." He nodded back towards the doorframe, and sure enough, her leather bag lay slouched on the floor.

"Thank you, Finn. I appreciate it," she said with a smile. "Are you sure I'm not imposing?"

He looked at her with mock offence.

"Megan, there is no such word as imposing in the Irish vocabulary," he said. His stern face broke into a teasing grin. "You're welcome here as long as you need it. Get yourself up and into the kitchen for some breakfast. I'm heading out for a bit. Got a call from a farmer about his sheep. I'm gonna head up there and do my veterinarian thing. Gotta pay the bills somehow! When I'm back, I'd love to show you around the place. Maybe take a walk in the woods and get some fresh air if the weather holds off?"

He looked at her expectantly from beneath dark lashes. Willing herself not to blush again, Megan nodded and smiled. "Sounds great! Thank you, Finn. Good luck with the sheep."

He smirked and turned on his heels, patting his leg as he left the room. Ted lifted his head and jumped down, padding out the door after his master.

"Good luck with the sheep?? Jesus, Megan," she quietly chided herself.

Sliding from the bed, she crossed the room to the door. They weren't big on closing doors around here, it seemed. With one hand on the frame, she stopped and listened.

The house around her seemed silent. It was crazy to think that there were so many occupants in the building and yet she could probably hear a pin if it dropped.

Music blasted from below her feet, and Megan jumped a little, startled by the sudden onset of noise within the house that had been as silent as a grave. With a nervous laugh, she closed the bedroom door. Lifting her handbag by the straps, she slung it across the room and plopped it on the bed. She hadn't had her phone in ages, and it was starting to weird her out that she had no idea what time it was. This must be what purgatory was like.

Pulling her wallet out of the way, she brushed past receipts and papers, rummaging deeper and deeper. No phone. It must be in the car.

Megan couldn't even remember the last time she had used it. Too much had happened, and her brain still felt like sludge after the ridiculously long sleep she'd had. With a sigh, she dumped everything back into the leather confines and dropped the bag by the bed. Time to get dressed and venture out. As she turned to grab her jeans from the floor, Megan gasped. A shadow was pressed against the window, hands tented against their face to better see in.

To see her.

She pulled a blanket from the bed to cover herself and raced towards the window. The figure darted away, but when she pressed her own face against the glass, she could clearly see Michael running off across the yard. A flock of chickens abandoned their pecking and scattered as he tore through them, his head thrown back in wild laughter.

Teenagers!

Megan rolled her eyes, the great humour she had been in dissolving into something a little cloudier. She pulled her clothes on, her skin crawling from her encounter with the teenage voyeur, and left the room.

10. Pretty, Young Stragglers

A soft breeze blew across the yard, picking up dead leaves and twirling them like dancers before dropping them to the rain-sodden ground again in its wake. Megan rubbed her arms to remove the gooseflesh that had broken out in the cold draft. She sat on the porch steps in front of the house, the late morning sunshine warm on her skin despite the persistent breeze. A small pebble dug into the soft flesh of her thigh, and she picked it out from beneath her jeans and flicked it across the yard.

Across the gravelled stretch, the garage doors stood open, upbeat Irish music drifting from within and mingling with the hushed lull of conversation.

Shay, Ollie, and Denny were inside, working on her car.

She hadn't met Denny yet. Hadn't even caught sight of him, but she had met another side to Shay over breakfast that morning. He had stood from the table to leave but when she walked in, he had dropped back into his seat and spent some time properly making her acquaintance.

That's what he had called it, anyway.

It had felt more like an interrogation to Megan.

An introvert, she still hadn't grown accustomed to the openness of the people here, and Shay had been the most probing yet. *Why was she in Ireland? How long had she planned on staying? Was she intending on meeting friends or family? What of her family back home? Did they not mind her taking off to galivant around a small country half the world away?*

Megan had fielded each question as it had come, but he had continued to fire them at her. Every now and then, he would stop and smile. She was sure it was meant to be a reassuring smile. A comforting one. But it was about as comforting as treading deep water while a shark circled below.

Starving, and more than a little disoriented from her long sleep, Megan had politely nibbled as she spoke, wishing he would stand up again and leave so she could eat in peace. At one point, her mouth full as she chewed, there had been a brief silence. Shay had sat watching her, waiting for her to respond to yet another question. She had tried to hold eye contact, hoping he would recognise how awkward she felt, but his gaze was too much, and she dropped her eyes. Ma had slapped a hand on the table hard, making her jump and almost choke on the piece of toast in her mouth.

"He asked you a question, young miss!" Ma had barked. "The polite thing to do is answer."

Embarrassed and uncomfortable with having so much direct attention focused on her, Megan had swallowed the lump of bread heavily, coughing as it slid down her throat.

"I'm sorry. I didn't want to speak with my mouth full."

Ma had stood, her hand still flat on the table as she glared at Megan. After a beat, she lifted it and limped back to the sink. Megan glanced at Shay, whose smug smirk rankled her. She pushed the plate away and continued to answer his questions. Eventually, he had either gleaned enough information from her or had grown bored, then with a scrape of his chair he pushed back from the table and left the room.

The silence that followed him was heavy until Ma broke it. "More tea, Megan, dear?" she chirped. Megan looked at her wide-eyed, unsure how to respond. The variety of moods among the Brogan family was giving her whiplash. She nodded and smiled, then surreptitiously pulled the plate closer to her, glad of the opportunity to eat in silence and without expectation.

She decided she didn't much like Shay after all.

The sound of tyres on gravel caught her attention. Her pulse quickened, anticipating Finn's return, the only consistently friendly face she had encountered so far in these mountains. Eager anticipation quickly turned to bewilderment as a police car rolled into view. Gardai, they called them here in Ireland, or just plain guards. The sun glinted off the sleek white body of the saloon car, the navy blue and luminous yellow decals making a statement of intent.

Her brow furrowed as Megan watched the car pull around in a wide arc. It came to a stop just metres from where she sat on the edge of the porch. The door swung open and a tall, bulky man unfolded himself from the driver's seat. He leaned against the open door, his arms resting casually across it as he studied her through tinted glasses. Frozen like a deer in headlights and unsure of what to do, Megan offered the stranger a faltering smile. His face lit up in response.

He stepped away from the car, slamming the door and pulled the shades from his face, slipping them into the shirt pocket of his uniform. The shirt was a pale blue with badges and patches that made no sense to her but were a familiar sight after her time in Dublin. The shirt was tucked into navy dress pants, a leather belt drawn tight and straining to hold everything in place. He wore no cap, though. Most of the guards she had seen on patrol always wore their hats. She relaxed slightly. Whatever this was, it wasn't official business.

"Well, hello there, young lady," he said cheerfully, slicking his flaming red hair back as he came to a stop in front of her. Megan squinted up at him, wishing he would move just a little to the right to shield her eyes from the sun. "You must be Megan."

He stretched out a hand and she took it, wincing as his giant paw held hers in a vise grip.

"Hi," she said. "I am Megan. Did the Brogans call you about the accident?"

As the words left her mouth, her heart rate increased again as she realised that she could be in trouble for not calling the guards immediately. For not calling them at all.

"They did call me. We Brogans like to keep each other up to date on any happenings, and you, my darling, would be considered a happening. These mountains are quiet. We don't often get stragglers in them, much less pretty, young stragglers like you."

He grinned again, but this time something slimy wriggled and writhed in Megan's gut. She pulled her hand from his and stood. "It's very nice to meet you . . ."

"Dominic," he answered. "Dominic Brogan. Shay is my brother, and this is our homeplace. This house has been in the Brogan family for generations." He stepped back and looked up at the house, pride etched on his face. "Our kin have been here since the time of the Great Hunger, possibly even before then!"

Megan looked at him, curiosity getting the best of her. "The Great Hunger?"

"The famine, my girl. Decimated this proud land. People had to do awful things to survive. They had to *become* awful things. There's not an Irish person alive today that hasn't been affected by it in some way. Something like that haunts a people for a long, long time. It becomes ingrained in your very bones. But I'm not here for a history lesson. Come! Let's go inside. You can stick the kettle on. The lads will know I'm here."

He nodded towards the car, which to be fair, stood out like a sore thumb among the rusted clunkers and the battered jeep that dotted the large yard.

"Oh. I was actually waiting on one of the guys to bring me my stuff from my rental car. I have nothing but the clothes on my back," she said with a nervous laugh. Megan didn't like the alarm bells that Dominic had set off inside her. She certainly didn't want to get stuck inside with him. Alone.

Once again, the absurdity of her situation dawned on her. What was she thinking? Taking up residence with veritable strangers, and all because one of them happened to smile at her a lot and was easy on the eye.

Behind her, the front door creaked. Ma stood just inside in the gloom.

"Come on, Megan, dear," she said, reaching a hand towards her. "You can help me with the tea." She smiled warmly at Megan, who turned to follow her inside. Ma turned to the large man on the steps. "Dominic," she said with a curt nod.

Megan watched with curious detachment as the warmth drained from Ma's eyes, only to be replaced by something akin to ice. Or fire. The old woman stood, cooly appraising her brother-in-law for a moment before turning on her heel and stalking into the house. Megan followed, glancing over her shoulder at Dominic.

His own eyes danced with amusement, and a smile spread across his face. He tipped his non-existent hat at her before moving away.

"I'll just go tell the men that the tea is on," he said, his body angling towards the garage. "I'll be sure to let them know you're waiting on your bags, Miss Megan." And with a throaty chuckle, he turned and loped away.

Shaking her head, perplexed by the odd encounter and the even odder exchange, she turned and followed Ma inside.

11. PILL BOTTLES SCATTERED

Megan sat on the bed, her face still creased in confusion. Her suitcase was open on the carpeted floor by her feet, an explosion of clothes spewing from its unzipped interior. Outside, the sun hid behind ominous-looking clouds that were dirty grey and heavy with the threat of rain. The dull weather mirrored her feelings.

After helping Ma with the tea earlier, she was surprised to discover that it was for the men only. She wasn't offered a cup. Wasn't even offered a chair to sit on.

She knew from many of the nights her dad spent reminiscing about Ireland that it still tended to be quite patriarchal, especially within the more traditional households. But seeing it in action left her feeling empty inside and more than a little uncomfortable. All the years she had spent as a child, a teenager, a young woman back home, comfortable in her freedom, yet within a couple of days here, she had been reduced to tea maker. It stung, and all of a sudden, she felt like maybe she understood Ma a little better.

No wonder the woman was so quiet most of the time, always shadowing the men and seeing to their needs. It was as though there was a quiet rage bubbling beneath the surface, and now any harsh words she had used against Megan previously felt softer around the edges. Megan felt a kinship with her, mostly borne from pity. Soon, she would be on her way, the freedom of the open road beckoning her. Every choice would be her own. But Ma would still be here. She would see out her days tucked away in the mountains surrounded by men, a servant to them all.

Yet, even with this newfound understanding, she was still hurt by the latest spat. She didn't know why Ma's harsh words stung more than anything any of the men had said to her so far. Maybe it was because understanding that made it feel worse. Maybe she secretly wanted Ma to know that Megan could see her. Really see her. She wanted Ma to like her, she realised.

Her relationship with her own mother had been strained for years.

It was no surprise, considering how happily her mother had swanned off to shack up and play house with her new boyfriend/former boss. The moment Eric's wife had found out about the affair and left, he had given Marcia the green light to replace her. Marcia had barely stopped to take a breath before she flung all her earthly possessions into a brand-new neon pink suitcase and tossed it into the back of Eric's Mercedes.

She had tousled her only daughter's hair as she passed her by, never looking back once as gravel sprayed and the Mercedes tore off down the street. Megan had always wondered why her dad had never fought Marcia on her decision, had never even moved from his armchair or dropped the book he was reading from in front of his face. As she grew older, though, she had come to realise that there had been no love left in the marriage.

Her dad had stayed for her alone, and her mother stayed only until a better option presented itself. She still remembered how her heart had begun to harden towards her mother as she'd stood on the pavement watching the shiny car ferry her away. She knew that had been the moment the maternal relationship began to wither and die. But in contrast, her relationship with her father blossomed from that day onward.

They had always been closer than Megan and Marcia, but a newfound understanding and appreciation of all he had endured for her had created a depth of love for her father that she hadn't thought possible.

Once her mother's shadow was gone from the house, it became a home. One filled with so much love and laughter, right up until the day she had come to find those empty pill bottles scattered on the bed sheets. Megan had never thought she needed a mother. Her dad had played both roles and played them well. Now, though, as she sat on a strange bed in a strange room, miles from home, she could see how subconsciously she had missed that maternal bond on some level. When Ma spoke kindly to her, as cliché as it was to say so, she felt warm and fuzzy inside. When Ma passed any sharp words or disapproving looks, they stung much more than they should from a practical stranger. This house, *this family*, it was all so insular. It was messing with her emotions in a way she still couldn't quite unravel.

As she had bustled around the kitchen with Ma, the large man in uniform, Dominic, questioned her as the men gathered for their tea.

Not unlike how Shay had that morning, but smoother.

His manner was easy and friendly, and while she felt much more at ease speaking to him as opposed to his brother, he still gave her that slithering feeling in her gut.

The sense of foreboding that gnawed at her, coupled with Ma's behaviour, had set her on edge. She had watched surreptitiously as Ma limped around the kitchen, fixing biscuits and scones, a pot of jam, butter, and tea, setting it all on the old table in front of the men as they talked over each other. Then Ma had slunk to the far corner of the kitchen, where she sat in the shadowed rocking chair. She didn't speak, didn't involve herself in the conversation at all. Dominic's presence seemed to simultaneously rattle her and spark something in her. The atmosphere in the gloomy room was so tense that Megan was sure she could have plucked a butter knife from the drawer and sliced it. Maybe serve it up to the men alongside their tea. Nobody else appeared to sense it but her.

And Dominic, who had cast his eyes towards the older woman every now and again, a small smile playing on his lips each time. Eventually, fed up with the constant questions, Megan had turned her back to him, asking Ma about using the shower. He had banged his cup on the table, and she turned back to him with a jolt. Dominic had gazed at her for a moment, his eyes dark and thoughtful, before smiling warmly and turning to join the conversation between Shay and Ollie.

Ma had quietly explained where the main bathroom was and how the shower worked. She told Megan that while she grabbed clean clothes from the case that Ollie had earlier deposited in her room, she would get clean towels and leave them in the bathroom for her, and that she was free to use any of the lotions and potions on the shelves, though the choices were limited. Megan had thanked her, smiling gratefully in what she hoped was a show of solidarity before leaving the room under the watchful gaze of the assembled men.

True to her word, when Megan made her way to the bathroom with a clean T-shirt and leggings under her arm, Ma had left two fluffy towels and a small washcloth on a low shelf for her. There was no sign of the woman herself. Loud voices continued to drift down the hallway from the kitchen, the conversation amongst the men still in full swing.

The room itself was odd.

It was a large bathroom by any standard and held a toilet, a sink, a mirrored vanity unit, a rack of shelves, and a shower, but the shower was walled off. It felt like the wash facilities in a gym or a high school shower block, which seemed completely at odds with the rest of what was a relatively standard bathroom, albeit a large one.

Flicking the small bolt closed, Megan was dismayed to see that it didn't fit very snugly in its place. It wouldn't take a whole lot for someone to get through. Then again, she had told herself, if she was worried about one of them breaking through the flimsy bathroom door after her, she had no business sleeping so soundly under the same roof. She tested the door to ensure it held, then turned the knob on the shower.

Steam curled lazily, filling the room as she rifled through the few products that littered the shelves haphazardly. Selecting a shower gel and shampoo, she was just about to turn away when she spied a small travel bottle of conditioner. Smiling to herself, Megan lifted the bottle. It was dusty and had clearly been forgotten about, which only served to alleviate any guilt she felt about using it. Her chestnut hair wasn't very long, falling just below her shoulders, but it was thick and practically impossible to manage without the help of some conditioner. Pleased with herself for spotting it, she placed her bottles inside the shower door and peeled off her clothes.

It felt good to rid herself of them. It seemed as though she had worn them for far too long and she couldn't wait to wash the grime from her body.

12. IT CAME FROM THE BASEMENT

After showering, Megan had dressed in a hurry, her eyes flicking towards the door. She brushed her teeth and bundled up her old clothes, reaching for the bolt to undo it.

But it was already undone.

As she pulled the knob, the door opened easily, and Megan felt a prickle along her spine. Had someone come in while she was showering? Had they watched her?

In the hallway outside, the basement door closed with an audible click.

Megan flung open the bathroom door, but of course, there was nobody there. She dashed to the safety of her room, drying and dressing in record time, that creeping uneasiness still lingering like cold fingers around the base of her spine.

By the time she had finished brushing the tangles from her hair, her heart rate had settled, and she plucked the sweaty, worn clothes from the floor to fold and tidy away with the rest of her small laundry pile in the bottom of the suitcase.

As she stowed the garments, something niggled at her. Something she was missing. And then it dawned on her.

Her underwear hadn't been among the small pile from the bathroom.

She remembered stripping them away because they were a pair that always amused her. Lemon yellow and covered in tiny lavender hearts and stars, they had been part of a multipack of black pants she had bought in a department store a couple of years back. She wasn't sure if the colourful underwear had ended up among the black ones by accident, but they amused her every single time she wore them.

And now they were gone.

And the bathroom door had been unlocked.

Could it have been Michael, the teenage voyeur? But then she remembered the sound of the basement door as it had closed. Denis? Or Denny, as they had referred to him. The son she had still to meet who, it seemed, spent all his time in the basement listening to loud music and watching horror movies. At least she hoped they were horror movies.

The memory of the scream that had drifted up through the kitchen floor the previous morning made her insides tighten.

She had only been a guest in the Brogan household for a little over twenty-four hours, yet somehow it felt longer.

Her underwear, though. Had he taken them?

Anger had begun to burn in her belly like fire, and without another thought, Megan marched from the bedroom to the kitchen, casting a hard glance at the basement door as she passed it, as though daring someone to appear through the wooden door.

The kitchen had fallen silent as she entered, all eyes on her. She knew she had probably been quite the sight, her face flushed red with annoyance, eyes wild as she scanned each face in the room.

And the anger had erupted from her in a fierce tirade as she ranted and raved about the younger Brogan watching her get dressed through the window, her underwear going missing from the previously locked bathroom, even her phone, which still hadn't turned up according to Ollie who claimed to have searched her rental car multiple times.

Nobody spoke as the frustration flowed like vomit from her, and as quickly as it had started, her tirade ended. The silence in the room and all those staring eyes had sucked the wind from her sails completely, and the angry flush was soon replaced by a burning embarrassment.

And then Ma had spoken.

Sharply and harshly, she had lain into Megan for daring to disrespect her family. The very family who had rescued her from the side of the road, fed her, and given her a bed, asking nothing in return. With every lash of the old woman's tongue, Megan felt tears prick her eyes until, eventually, they spilled over. She mumbled an apology, then turned and fled. The room had exploded with laughter on her departure, the sound echoing against the walls and following her down the hallway and back into the room where she buried her head in the pillow, crying hot tears until her body felt like a dried-up husk.

Now she sat on the edge of the bed, her head in her hands, unsure of what to do.

Slowly, a sound seeped through the murkiness that swirled in her mind. Megan lifted her face and listened intently.

Someone was crying.

It was the same ghostly sound that had plagued her the previous night, but this time curiosity got the better of her. Lifting herself from the bed quietly, Megan moved around the room, following the sound towards the dresser. She dropped to her knees and moved along the carpet. Beneath the dresser, an old-fashioned vent was set into the wall, the edges of the paper curling around it. Whoever had papered the walls of the room had done a pretty shoddy job. It looked as though the vent had originally been papered over, but time had pulled the paper away, revealing the slats that the muffled sobbing was coming from.

Megan knew instantly that the sound was travelling up from the basement.

Another of the mysterious Denny's movies?

She hoped so, but a sense of disquiet had settled over her.

Megan lifted herself from the floor, her knees cracking as she stood. She dusted off her leggings and crawled onto the bed. A headache was beginning to announce itself, the band of tightness wrapping around her temples and forehead like a bad omen. A tension headache. The kind she always suffered from after any kind of confrontation.

Fatigue fell across her like a weighted blanket. Pulling the covers over her body, Megan consoled herself with the knowledge that a short nap would certainly help the thumping pain in her head, if not cure it entirely.

Closing her eyes, she willed herself to unconsciousness. The soft crying continued to travel through the vent. It followed her into the darkness as sleep finally took her.

13. WHO COULD SAY NO TO ALL THIS FRESH AIR

"Ah, don't mind Ma too much. She gets fierce protective about her boys. Especially Michael, since he's the baby of the family."

Finn smiled at her, his eyes full of mischief. Megan offered a small smile in return. She knew that he was probably just trying to make her feel a little better about everything that had transpired earlier that day, but she also knew that he was probably right. She was a stranger here, and she probably wouldn't be very accommodating herself to a stranger who pointed fingers and fired accusations at her own loved ones. It wasn't like she had any proof. And it wasn't like she had broached the subject calmly.

He held out his hand to her. "Best just to chalk it up to emotions and move on. Ma doesn't really hold grudges. And she likes you."

Megan's smile widened as she grabbed his hand and hauled herself across the huge tree trunk. It lay across the forest floor, its massive width covered in silvery moss and an abundance of tiny white mushrooms packed together in tight clusters. It pleased her to hear him say that Ma liked her. The woman was so difficult to read, it was nice to hear something positive from someone who knew and understood her.

With only a slight wobble, Megan found her balance on the broad trunk and sucked in a deep lungful of air. The rain had continued to hold off, and the sun shone down, but it was weak, with no real warmth. The air was crisp and heavy with the scent of pine and wild garlic. From their vantage point high in the forest, the surrounding mountains spread out before the pair. Megan's eyes swept back and forth across the landscape as she drank in the vista.

Rolling hills swept downwards into valleys dotted with green fields and snaking grey ribbons of road that disappeared and reappeared behind the distant hedgerows and stands of trees. The sun shimmered off a lake, its glimmering edges just visible, a great distance away. At their backs, the forest soared upward, skeletal fingers reaching desperately towards the promises held by the blue sky. It was breathtaking.

Being out in the forest reminded Megan so much of time spent outdoors with her dad growing up. He had always insisted on spending time in nature. "Nothing will prepare you for life like nature will," he would say as he pointed out flora and fauna. He always made an extra effort to teach her about anything that occurred naturally in both the forests near their home back in the States and the woods that surrounded his birth home back in Ireland. It delighted her to see so many familiar things here. It was like a little piece of home in a strange land.

A little piece of her dad.

Overhead, soft white clouds skated by, but in the distance, storm clouds had begun to gather again. The reprieve from the storm would only be a short one.

Feeling his eyes on her, Megan turned to look at Finn.

He winked before jumping from the tree trunk, offering his hand again. With a smirk, Megan jumped down without his help. She'd teach these Brogan men yet that not all women needed a man to feel capable.

"Whoa! Watch your step!" Finn pulled her sharply away from the direction she was taking.

Looking around in confusion, Megan raised her eyebrows at him. Finn moved carefully towards the place she had stood. Reaching out, he plucked a thin branch from the ground, then tossed it a few feet from where she had just been.

CRACK!

Megan's heart leapt as the sound reverberated through the forest. The trees surrounding them came alive as flocks of birds took flight, startled by the loud noise.

Finn glanced across his shoulder at her gravely. "Badger trap. Stand in one of those and you'll break an ankle at the very least."

Megan nodded. Her face drained of colour.

Finn turned back towards her and moved through the trees. Megan followed, throwing a last glance over her shoulder at the toothy metal trap that she had almost stepped in moments ago.

As they walked among the trees, they spoke easily, as though they had known each other all their lives. Compared to the rest of his family, Finn was very easy company to be in, and Megan appreciated it.

She spoke about her life back in America, surprising herself by telling him about her troubled family history. He let her speak but sensed when it was becoming too much. With a smooth deftness, he turned the conversation to her father, as though recognising him as a safe topic. They spoke of her father's affinity to this island that birthed him, and Finn listened eagerly as she spoke of her plans for whenever she got back on the road.

"I reckon the storm will slow progress with your car," he said, glancing across at her, concern on his face. "The lads will do their best to get you moving quickly, but no guarantees with the weather they seem to be promising us. It's looking like a rough one. To be honest, though, it'd be nice to have you around for a few days. I like your company."

A smile creased her face despite how hard she tried to hide it, and it only grew as she watched his concern wash away to relief.

"I guess I could extend my stay by a few days." She smiled, nudging him in the ribs. "Who could say no to all this fresh mountain air, anyway?"

The ground soon started to decline beneath their feet, and soon the Brogan homestead became visible once more. Megan turned to look back upon the path they had walked, sad to leave the wild terrain. She'd have to try to get out here again before she left, but definitely not alone.

As the memory of the steel trap entered her mind, her eyes caught a flash of colour between the trees far back on the path they had just walked. She grasped at Finn's sleeve, her eyes wide, as she watched the man in the yellow raincoat step out of the cover of the forest. He stopped dead in the middle of the path, watching them.

Finn turned, a sound akin to a growl escaping his lips when he saw Liam O'Keefe standing there. "Fuck off and mind your own business, O'Keefe," he roared.

Megan held her breath, her pulse thrumming as she waited to see what would happen next. There was clearly no love lost between the Brogans and this man.

The man she had nearly flattened with her rental car.

The seconds felt as though they lasted an eternity, but seconds they were. The man turned and disappeared back into the tree line, the bright yellow of his raincoat visible as he moved away until, eventually, he was swallowed by the sea of trees.

"Fucking spacer," growled Finn, as he slowly started back down the trail towards the house. He glanced across at Megan and smiled.

She knew he was trying to put her at ease, and to be fair, it was working. The further away the O'Keefe man had gotten, the better she'd felt. With Finn so close to her side, she felt safe, even in this unfamiliar place filled with unfamiliar people.

Every now and then, their fingers would brush lightly against one another. Electricity sparked between them, conversation dying away to stolen glances and full smiles. Just as they passed beneath the archway of hedges that separated the Brogan land from the forest, the heavens opened, and rain began to bucket down upon them.

Megan shrieked as the cold rain hit her, needling her face and soaking her almost instantly. Finn laughed cheerfully and grabbed her hand.

He pulled her through the downpour, steering her towards the closest building. Pulling the barn door aside, he pushed her through the dark opening and followed directly behind. He wrenched the door back on its hinges, leaving it open just enough for a hint of dreary evening light to seep through the crack. The rain poured down relentlessly, drowning out almost everything.

Megan peered through the door, watching as puddles formed quickly, turning to lakes and then rivers across the wide yard. The only sound she could hear beyond the drumming of water against the ground and the old wooden structure that protected them now was her own laboured breath from the quick dash against the sudden onslaught.

Turning away from the door, her breath caught in her throat. Finn stood inches from her, his eyes dark and brooding. Her stomach fluttered as she gazed back at him, and in an instant, he was on her, mouth and hands seeking her out.

He pushed her roughly against the wooden walls, further into the shadows. A small moan escaped her as one hand pinned her arms behind her back and the other moved across her T-shirt before disappearing beneath it.

But it was over as suddenly as it had begun. One minute, their bodies were so close they were practically the same person, the next, an ocean of space appeared between them as Finn stepped back, releasing her from his grip.

Megan almost stumbled without his arms pinning her. She stared at him, panting, unsure of what had just happened. Finn gazed back, the shadows moving across his face, rendering it impossible to read.

"I'm sorry," he gasped. "I shouldn't have done that."

He turned and disappeared through the crack in the door, leaving Megan alone in the barn, speechless. Her mind reeled as she watched him jog across the yard and disappear around the side of the house.

The memory of his hands on her skin, rough but somehow tender at the same time, made her breath catch in her throat. She had never felt so turned on and so confused at the same time, and she was aghast to find tears pricking her eyes for the second time that day.

Something nuzzled against her hand, and Megan jumped, shrieking as she fell back against the wall.

Ted rubbed his furry brown body against her legs, his tail whipping back and forth in a frenzy.

Megan sank to the cold ground, bits of dried hay sticking through her thin leggings like daggers. She pulled the dog close, burying her face in his fur. His coat was dry. He must have taken shelter in here, too, she realised as she stroked his ears.

She sat cradling the dog's head on her lap, mindlessly running her fingers through his fur. As the rain started to ease just a little, she stood and dusted herself down before dashing across the yard and into the house. The dog followed loyally, padding down the hallway behind her as she crept towards the guest room.

Not even Finn's raucous laughter spilling from the kitchen turned the dog's head as he followed his new best friend.

14. Lauren Runs

*B*ranches whipped against her face as she ran deeper into the woods. The stinging pain barely registered. Only one thought raced through her mind like a repeating banner.

Freedom.

Her lungs burned and her heart thudded painfully in her chest as she raced through the dark thickets of trees. Not so long ago, she would have run from the darkness in search of the light. In search of safety.

Now, though, the only safety for her was within the writhing mass of shadows that she ran blindly towards. That was where she would find sanctuary, however temporary.

As she bolted through the dense growth, trees looming over her like silent, dark sentinels, her ears strained to hear any sound beyond her laboured breath and the snap and crack of twigs beneath her bare feet.

The woods were ominously silent.

As she crashed through the undergrowth, it crossed her mind that it might be best to move silently, but her hammering heart and the fear that had lodged itself at the base of her spine wouldn't allow the thought to gain any traction.

Suddenly in the distance, dogs began to bark, and she knew they were trailing her. Using the damn dogs to locate their prey for them.

No wonder they had been so obliging, allowing her to spend time with the stupid mutts. The canines' mindless adoration of anyone who paid attention to them had been the only joy in all the wretched days she had spent in captivity, but now they would easily pick up her scent and follow her to the ends of the earth, no doubt.

"Idiot!" she berated herself.

She moved like the wind, like her life depended on her escape. And she knew very well that it did.

CRACK!

A white-hot pain seared her ankle, and she tumbled to the ground. Shrieking and writhing, she tried in vain to get moving again, but something had her pinned in place.

She froze as a branch broke to her left.

As the darkness around her suddenly brightened, she covered her eyes to shield herself from the blazing light.

Still, in the distance, the dogs barked.

With a whimper, she dared to glance from behind the pathetic safety of her slender forearm. To her surprise, it was a familiar face, one not altogether unwelcome.

"You!" she hissed. "Don't just stand there. Help me!"

The man stood unmoving behind the torch, most of his features obscured by its blinding glare. There was no denying it was him, though. That bright yellow coat wrapped around his long, lean frame. The scar on his face. That mop of wild curls.

"Help me!" she hissed again. Sweat was beginning to bead on her brow, her lower leg pulsing with pain. "Or at least take that fucking light out of my eyes. You're burning a hole through my retinas."

At her request, the light swung down towards the ground, and she moaned as metal glinted. Her ankle was caught in a steel trap.

"Is that a fucking animal trap?" she asked, hysteria rising in her voice.

"Aye. 'Tis."

She glanced from his defeated face to the jagged metal teeth that had shredded her flesh, and back again. It was all beginning to make sense.

The day she had first seen him, way back before this nightmare had begun, the man before her appeared from the trees that lined the old country road she had found herself on. Despite the vibrant yellow coat, she was none the wiser to his presence until he had stepped from the woods.

"Come to my house," he had said. "You can use our phone to call someone."

She didn't consider herself stupid or naïve. She had watched enough horror movies back home with her friends to know it was a bad idea.

Figuring he was some backwoods weirdo with cannibalistic tendencies, she had turned his offer down and moved quickly and warily away from him, and towards the distant lights that pierced the leafy darkness like fireflies. The familiar blue lights grew closer, and she felt immeasurably relieved.

Police meant safety.

What was she thinking anyway, coming out here at night? That had been a risky move all the way out here in the mountains. She'd get the police car to drop her back and accept her punishment.

A shudder ran through her as that particular punishment flashed in her mind.

Still, as bad as it was, she knew now that it was better than what she had gone through in this place. With these monsters.

Gritting her teeth, she moved towards the patrol car lights.

"You don't want to do that." The panic in his voice had given her pause, but she eyed him warily, nonetheless. "You won't be safe with them."

"I'll take my chances," she had replied as she turned towards her false salvation.

The man said no more to her but had stood in the road and watched her progression.

As the patrol car pulled up alongside her, she'd looked over her shoulder and watched as he melted back into the darkness, like he belonged there. Lucky escape, *she thought.*

How wrong she had been.

"You tried to help me."

He nodded; the movement barely perceptible but for the shadows that betrayed it.

"You seemed like a nice girl. I know what happens to pretty girls that step through the Brogans' door," he spat. "They don't come back out again."

"So help me now!" she pleaded, wincing as she tried to move closer. The stinging weight of the steel trap around her ankle prevented her from getting very far.

The light clicked off suddenly, darkness rushing in to swallow her once more.

A twig snapped again, ahead of where she lay slumped among the rotting leaves and forest debris.

"Can't do that," he replied from a greater distance than before. "Us O'Keefes have had an agreement with the Brogans for a long, long time.

Long before me. If I can save 'em first, well and good. And if I can't, well, then they're fair game and none of my business no more. I don't like it. My da always said I don't have to like it, but I have to deal with it. See this scar?" He gestured in the dark, and though she couldn't see his face anymore, she remembered the jagged lesion that marred his skin. *"They did that to me for breaking the rules before. They don't just hurt pretty girls, you know."*

Her body started to shake uncontrollably. The first hot tears traced a path along her face as she began to cry.

"Please help me," she sobbed. *"You have no idea what they've done to me. Or what they'll do when they find me."*

Leaves rustled as the man moved back into the forest slowly.

"Oh, I know, alright. They're monsters," he called back gently. *"I'm sorry."*

"At least tell me your name," she whispered.

"Liam."

The rustling quickened before dying away, and she was alone again. Not for long, though, she knew, as the distant barking closed in and changed to an incessant howling.

In a final desperate attempt to free herself, she pulled at the metal snare, biting her lips until they bled in an attempt to cage the scream that burned in her throat. The metal teeth scraped against bone and her ankle throbbed as fresh blood pumped from the wound, soaking through the leaves and into the forest floor.

The sound of heavy footsteps surrounded her, and as a warm, furry body collided with her fragile one, she knew her time was up.

Still, she clawed manically at the snare.

"Well, well, boys. We found ourselves a little runaway."

A chorus of sneers and laughter followed.

She pulled in a breath, the heady scent of pine and wild garlic filling her lungs. An anguished howl, one filled with rage and pain and sorrow, erupted from her, piercing the cold night air.

One of the men lashed out quickly, silencing her scream.

As the barking of the dogs faded in and out, the larger of the men released the snare as another hauled her from the ground and tossed her across his shoulders. Her whole body tensed as pain flared, and she screeched in agony. She flopped back down, her body turning limp as she surrendered to the blissful ignorance of blackness.

Still, though, the larger man's words penetrated her muddled confusion and broke her heart as she dangled from the arms of her captor.

"She's a hazard now. It's time to get her down to the basement."

15. SICK OF THIS ROOM

The rain continued to thunder down in unrelenting sheets. The sky was dull, swollen with dirty grey clouds, and in the distance, thunder rumbled. Megan had lain on the small iron bed, her mind playing and replaying the earlier events with Finn.

She thought of how he had been as they strolled through the forest. His eyes alive with childlike excitement as he showed her different flowers and plants or pointed at different sights in the distance. That image of him would suddenly become overlain in her mind by the image of him in the barn where they had taken shelter. His eyes dark, full of lust and something else too. How roughly he had pushed her and moulded her to his will. Until whatever had taken over him disappeared. He had run and left her, and she wasn't sure how she even felt about it. There was no denying the attraction between them, but the Finn she encountered in the shadows of the barn was not the Finn she had slowly come to know. It scared her and excited her in equal measure.

Her fingers stroked Ted's ears absentmindedly, and the dog snored, deeply asleep and content where he lay curled behind Megan's knees on the bed. As the day wore on, the shadows lengthened, and with a sigh, Megan pushed herself from the bed. She flicked on the lamp, its soft glow illuminating the room. She stood for a moment and gazed out the window at the unrelenting rain. The house around her had been as silent as a grave but appeared to be coming to life. Doors opened and closed along the hallway, hushed conversations that she couldn't quite make out drifted through the house, haunting it like ghosts.

Megan realised that among the regular household sounds, she was straining her ears for the sounds of crying.

Her eyes flicked down towards the wallpaper-covered vent, but it was silent.

Movement beyond the window caught her attention, and she watched as two shapes drifted among the pig pens. They were well wrapped up against the driving rain, but she could tell by the lithe movements that one of them was Finn. As though sensing her there, he stopped and turned. Embarrassed to be caught staring at him through the window, Megan tugged at the curtains, pulling them across. It wasn't like there was much light out there to begin with. Mortification needled at her then. Why did she close the curtains? He probably thought she was some lovesick idiot. Or thought she was annoyed with him for his behaviour earlier. Was she annoyed? She wasn't quite sure herself how she felt about it.

Throwing herself back onto the bed with a grunt, Megan shimmied back into a comfortable position. Ted lifted his head, his soulful brown eyes gazing at her, waiting for her to settle so he could return to his snoozing. She patted his head and lay back against the pillows.

She was bored and she was sick of sitting in this room, but this didn't feel like the type of house she could just wander freely. She still hadn't met the elusive Denny, but she'd spied the grandfather again on her way out of the bathroom earlier. The old man was being helped back to his room by Ollie, whose eyes roved along her body. It made her flesh crawl, and she had seriously considered a shower after it, but the unbolted door that morning had been enough to put her off spending extended periods of time in the bathroom.

Her eyes wandered around the room, taking in any new detail she had previously missed, although at this point there was very little left for her to discover here.

And then she saw it.

16. WHO IS Lauren?

It was the shimmer that caught her eye.

The soft lamplight glinted off it, and she moved her head this way and that, mesmerised by it. Megan stood again. On the bed, Ted grumbled in that way dogs do when they're fed up with humans. She crept forward, her eyes never leaving the space where the light reflected off whatever was caught against the peeling wallpaper. It was behind the door, practically invisible to anyone unless they happened to be lying on the bed. In the dark. With the lamp on.

Just as she had been.

Megan knew this room had been largely unused before she arrived here. Ma had said as much, and the thin coating of dust told of half-hearted attempts to keep the room clean without any real commitment to its upkeep.

With trembling fingers, she grasped the curling seam of wallpaper between her finger and thumb and lifted it away from the wall. With a gentle tinkle, whatever had been lodged there fell to the carpet.

It was a necklace.

Dropping to her knees, Megan lifted the thin chain and let it unspool into her open palm. The chain was silver, and on the attached pendant was a name.

Lauren.

Megan studied it, held it up to the light and examined it, as though it would begin speaking at any moment and explain itself.

What was it doing hidden behind the wallpaper? And who had put it there in the first place? *Who was Lauren?*

There was a knock beside her.

Megan jumped to her feet and turned as the door opened, the whisper of wood across the carpet sounding much louder than it actually was within the deathly quiet space.

Ollie's auburn head peered around the door, his eyes narrowing.

"What are you doing behind there?" he asked.

"Nothing," Megan replied. "Was just stretching myself out after lying down all afternoon."

Ollie continued looking at her, the narrowed eyes smoothing out as a sly smile crept onto his face. His eyes moved, scanning the entirety of her body.

Megan felt exposed. Uncomfortable.

"Ma said to tell you dinner is almost ready. She wants a hand setting everything up."

With that, he turned and left the room. It hadn't been a question or a request. It had been an order, and that knowledge did nothing except increase the discomfort that Megan felt. Why did this family make her feel so uncomfortable in her own skin?

She resolved there and then to leave the Brogan household tomorrow.

If her car wasn't ready, well, she'd just use the phone to call a cab. Or maybe one of them would be in a good enough humour to drop her to the nearest town. She could worry about retrieving the car once she was away from the dark clouds that hung perpetually over this place. Both literally and figuratively right now. She was aware all at once of the rain still hammering against the window, and the necklace squeezed tight in her closed fist. Lifting her hand from where she had hidden it behind her back, Megan looked at the necklace once more, her finger gently tracing the letters of the name.

Who are you?

Glancing around the room for somewhere safe to keep it – away from prying eyes – her eyes landed on her suitcase, and she moved towards it. But then Megan stopped.

She still hadn't found her phone.

She had a sneaking suspicion her phone had been right where she thought it was but that somebody else had gotten their hands on it. She couldn't lock the room door, and she was pretty sure that some of the people in the house weren't averse to going through her things.

The unbolted bathroom door and missing underwear entered her mind again, and with a shudder she reached for the pillow on the bed. Stuffing her arm inside, she buried the necklace into the furthest corner of the pillowcase and dropped the pillow back in place.

"MEGAN!"

She flinched at the sound of her own name. She was being called like a dog to go help serve the men. What a fucked-up system this family had in place. Still, she wasn't brave enough to defy Ma's call. Megan sighed, her shoulders sagging, and left the room. She didn't even bother to close the door behind her.

It wasn't like it would make a difference.

As she moved along the hall, Megan noticed that the crying was back. She hadn't heard it in her room, or hadn't been aware of it, but now it was just barely audible beneath the other distant sounds in the house. She stopped and peered around her.

Then froze.

The basement door just ahead was open. She could feel a draught curl around her ankles, could smell the stale, earthy air that emanated from the opening. Stepping closer, moving as silently as possible, Megan peered into the blackness.

There was no light, and the hallway bulb did little to penetrate the darkness within. She could see the start of a staircase that led down, further into the void. She moved closer until she stood right in the doorway. The sobbing floated up to her, climbing each wooden step to assault her senses. Why would anyone be down there in the darkness?

It was a little clearer here than it sounded when it came through the vent in her room.

Definitely a woman.

And she sounded young.

The anguished sobs, muffled though they were, tore at Megan's heart. It didn't just sound like someone scared or in pain – although both were evident in the cries – it sounded like hopelessness. Moving forward, further into the dark, Megan paused for a moment.

Should she go down? Should she go get someone?

Before she could make a decision, a face appeared in the darkness before her, pale and horrible.

Megan screamed as hands grasped at her.

17. Nice to Finally Meet You, Megan

As the hands pulled at her, drawing her further into the darkness, Megan was aware of a cacophony of voices in the hallway behind her. Among the shouts and excitement, only one sentence stood out.

"Are we doing this now?"

She had no clue who uttered those words, but they stuck in her brain, and her screams ratcheted higher. The rest of her body shut down, though, and she froze in place, unable to either run or fight.

And then she was in the light again.

Her body sank to the carpet. She shook uncontrollably as strong arms wrapped around her. She smelled pig shit and sweat and a hint of cologne and knew it was Finn who comforted her. He caught her chin between his fingers and lifted her face to his.

"Megan, it's okay. Calm down. It was just Denny messing with you. Calm down, darling."

She looked at him with wide, frightened eyes. Slowly the scene came back into focus.

She sat crumpled on the floor with Finn crouched by her side. Shay watched quietly while Ollie and young Michael tittered and joked quietly between themselves, amusement evident on their faces. A big man with skin so pale it was almost translucent stood in the basement doorway, neither in darkness nor light. He watched her, a smile playing on his thin lips. Something ugly swam behind his eyes and Megan found herself moving a little closer to Finn.

Beyond them all, Ma stood silently against the wall.

Her head was bowed, and she watched the scene from behind hard eyes. Her face was expressionless through it all. She didn't look amused by Megan's outburst, nor did she look concerned for the frightened girl. Megan watched as the woman lifted herself away from the wallpaper and moved quietly back up the hall towards the kitchen.

The pale man stepped forward, tucking unruly hair behind his ears. His hair was neither dark like Finn's nor the auburn colour of the other men. It was the same fiery red as the man who had visited earlier. Shay's brother, Dominic. The guard.

He stretched out a hand towards her, the same sly grin still on his face.

"Apologies. I was only having the craic with you. Nice to finally meet you, Megan."

Finn narrowed his eyes at his brother and slapped his hand away. He stood and reached for Megan, helping her to stand. "You're a fucking eejit, Denny. Look at her! You've scared her half to death!"

Behind them, Shay grew bored and moved away. The two younger men still whispered and giggled, amused at the show as it continued to play out before them. With a supportive arm around her waist, Finn led Megan up the hall towards the kitchen.

"I just wanted to show her my basement. She's gonna see it anyway." Denny giggled.

Finn stopped and turned to his brother. His eyes flashed with barely concealed rage and anger radiated from him, reminding Megan once more of the "other" Finn she had encountered in the barn.

"Stay the fuck away from her," hissed Finn before turning on his heels.

The pale man's laughter followed them up the hall and into the kitchen, only disappearing when the basement door slammed shut.

18. NOTHING LIKE a PIG TO DISPOSE OF UNWANTED THINGS

"Clear those plates and get the kettle on, Ma. Actually, on second thought, I'm sure our esteemed guest wouldn't mind helping out. What do you say, Megan?"

Shay looked at Megan expectantly.

A forkful of food hovered in front of her mouth, but the finality with which he'd spoken, coupled with the laser stare from Ma, made Megan lower the fork and sigh.

Women really were second-class citizens in this household.

The men had cleared their plates quickly and noisily as she had delicately picked her way around her own plate, conscious of being watched. It was as though Ollie, Michael, and Shay had a silent pact to take turns staring at her while she ate, and it made Megan uncomfortable. She was introverted at the best of times, but this family had put her on edge so many times that her nerves were shot.

Now, they had all pushed their empty, bloodstained plates away from them, towards the centre of the table. Megan hadn't been able to bring herself to eat much of the steak. Rare meat wasn't her thing at all, and it had sickened her to watch the men tuck so heartily into the pink slabs, dribbles of crimson juice running from chin to table as they sported mouthfuls of masticated meat while they conversed across the table. Even the greasy, scarlet pools that remained on the plates were turning her stomach. It made it easier to push her own plate away. Shay pulled a packet of smokes from his shirt pocket and lit up right there at the table. He blew the first plume of smoke directly towards her, and Megan coughed and waved the cloud away.

But she hadn't dared say anything to him.

He had stared at her, his eyes silently challenging her, and he seemed almost disappointed when she lowered her head and broke eye contact.

She pushed back from the table, gathering plates and carrying them towards the sink. To her surprise and quiet delight, Finn stood from the table to help.

"What are you doing, Finn?" Shay asked. "That's woman's work."

Finn barely glanced at his father as he pulled a bucket from beneath the sink and gestured for Megan to scrape the plates into it. "Would you ever stop? Someone has to feed the pigs. It's not like you'll get up off your hole and do it."

Ollie and Michael sniggered but were silenced quickly by a sharp look from Shay. The two stood and slunk from the room, whispers and titters of laughter following them down the hall. Megan started to wash the dishes, smiling at Finn as he plucked a towel from the drawer and dried each item.

Behind them, Shay tutted and pushed his chair back noisily before leaving the kitchen.

"Finn, honey, leave those and I'll help Megan. Why don't you go watch the hurling with your da and the lads in the sitting room. I'll bring the tea in shortly."

Ma looked uncomfortable and hovered around her son. Megan watched the woman's eyes flick from Finn's face to the towel in his hands, like she couldn't quite work out how such an alien item had come into his possession. Only when he smiled and swatted at her with the towel did Ma relax, her shoulders visibly slumping.

She pulled the towel from Finn's hands and swatted him back playfully. "Go on, the pair of you. Go show Megan the pigs," she said, a small smile playing on her lips.

Finn leaned down and kissed her cheek. "Cheers, Ma."

With the bucket almost full of leftover food from throughout the day hanging by his side, Finn grabbed Megan's hand with his free one and pulled her from the kitchen and through the front door. They laughed as they ran together around the side of the house, like two children on the hop from school.

It felt that way, though, Megan realised. Like she was shirking some responsibilities that she had never signed up for. The Brogan effect.

She had become too accepting too quickly of the expectations the Brogan men had of her. Of women, in general. Within a couple of days, she had become a bow-headed woman, almost reverential in the presence of the Brogan patriarchy. When they called, she came. When they told her to do something, she did it without argument. It dawned on her how frighteningly quick this change had come about. She had never been one to argue her point much, but she was also nobody's workhorse. Least of all, these strangers.

She vowed there and then to assert herself more for the remainder of her time with the family. She was very grateful for the hospitality they had shown her, but she could still be assertive in a polite way.

The rain had eased to a light drizzle, though the prominence of dark storm clouds in the sky promised no end to the bad weather. The ground was soaked, and Megan found herself giggling like a child as they picked their way around the miniature rivers and lakes that had formed in the yard. Finn laughed mischievously over his shoulder at her before stomping his heel in a puddle as he jumped it. Megan squealed as cold water splashed up around her. She yelled his name in childish glee.

As they rounded the corner, she noticed a cellar door set into the ground.

"Does that lead to the basement too?" she asked, pointing at the sealed entrance.

Finn turned to look and nodded. "Aye," he said. "As much as I love the pigs, we do have to butcher them from time to time for food. We rely heavily on our own land and produce. There's a cold room kitted out down there. Ma would kill us if we carried carcasses through the house, so that's how they get inside."

He smiled at her, and Megan was aware that the one she returned was small and not very genuine. She wasn't stupid. She knew animals died to feed people. Hell, she was a big fan of a double cheeseburger herself. Hearing the process being spoken about so casually stirred something in her, though. Animals were so innocent.

It was always innocence that got brutalised.

As they approached the pens, the smell of wet mud and pig shit intermingled with the smell of the animals. It wasn't the sweetest smell, but it wasn't altogether unpleasant either. The yard was alive with sounds. Rustling and grunting, squeals and yelps, each sound fought to be heard above the next.

With a whistle and click of Finn's tongue, a small mass of bodies detached from the shadows of the little shed that sat in the corner of the largest pen.

With excited squeals, the pigs rushed in their direction, and Megan ran towards the low stone wall with delight. As she leaned across, Finn grabbed her by the elbow and pulled her back.

"Whoa!" He laughed. "Take it easy! I know they're pretty delightful, but pigs can be dangerous animals. Especially when they know it's feeding time!"

Megan stepped back, mildly chastised but still entranced by the animals.

She hadn't spent much time in the countryside in her life, and she rarely saw animals that weren't domesticated household pets. Dogs, cats, hamsters . . . sure, she'd seen plenty of those. But she didn't think she'd seen a real live pig since she last visited a petting zoo. She hadn't been to one of those since she was just a child.

Tossing the contents of the bucket over the wall, Finn stood back and watched as the creatures grunted and squealed, butting the others out of the way until they were each content with their own patch of food.

Without taking his eyes from the pigs, he reached out a hand and pulled Megan closer to the wall. Closer to him. He pointed at the pigs, introducing her to each one.

"That's Chris P. Bacon," he said, and Megan snorted.

"You called your pig Crispy Bacon?" she asked, one eyebrow cocked in amusement.

"Chris P. Bacon," he said again, enunciating each syllable. "And that's his brother, Kevin."

Megan howled with laughter, doubling over until her sides ached. Finn watched her, amused.

"I'm sorry," she said as she straightened up and wiped tears from her eyes. "Go on. Tell me who the rest of them are."

Finn looked at her deadpan. Then his face split into a huge smile and he turned back towards the snuffling pigs, pointing at each one in turn.

"Hammibal Lector. Albert Einswine. Tommy Hillpigger. That big girl there is their mother, Honey D. Hamm. Oh, and that one is Sausage."

When he looked back at Megan, she was creased almost in half beside him, laughing so hard that she struggled to breathe. He stood watching her until she straightened back up, a half-smile on his face. Megan wiped at her teary eyes, her mouth still twitching and her stomach aching from her laughter.

"They're great pig names. Especially Sausage," she said matter-of-factly. Then she caught Finn's eye and they both broke into fresh peals of laughter, leaning against each other in their mirth.

And then a voice materialised right by her ear and Megan gasped with fright.

"If you were to end up in that pen at the wrong time, they'd gobble you up in about ten minutes," Denny said. He pulled deep on a cigarette, the tip flaring orange, then deep red, before dulling again. A thin plume of smoke escaped him and travelled into the darkening sky where it was swallowed by the drizzle that continued to fall from the heavens. "All that would be left is your teeth, hair, and nails. Nothing like a pig to dispose of unwanted things."

Megan stepped back, wanting to put distance between herself and the large man. His presence, the way he watched her from behind dead eyes . . . it all turned the blood in her veins to ice.

He turned to Finn. "Da was asking where you'd got to with the chief dishwasher. How about you get her back inside and in front of the sink where she belongs." He looked at Megan with a cold smirk and she bristled.

"How about you go fuck yourself," she spat, shocked by the venom in her own words.

Stars burst behind her eyes and Megan found herself sprawled in the mud. She tasted blood in her mouth. Putting her fingers to her lip, she winced at the stinging pain she felt.

There was blood on her fingers.

Tears pricked her eyes as she looked up at Denny in shock. He loomed over her, still as a snake and just as deadly.

He jabbed a finger towards Finn. "Get her back inside. Now."

And then he turned and walked away, the shadows swallowing his swaggering gait almost instantly.

Finn looked at her helplessly, then reached out and lifted her from the dirt.

"C'mon," he said quietly, not looking her in the eye. "Let's get you into some dry clothes. It's probably too wet to be hanging around out here in the dark anyway."

She leaned on him, more from need than want, her legs still like jelly as the gravity of what had happened seeped into her bones like marrow. *Get her back inside. Now.*

As they moved towards the front of the house, something rustled in the trees behind them. Finn, lost in thoughts of his own, took no heed. Twigs cracked and broke, and Megan turned her head to see.

A flash of yellow raincoat between the trunks caught her eye as Finn steered her around the corner and towards the front door.

The only door.

There's only one door. That information seemed somehow important, but shock and pain still clouded her mind and made it difficult to grasp anything concrete. They climbed the steps to the porch and Finn pulled the door open. Then it hit her like a sledgehammer.

Only one way in and out.

Only one escape.

19. YOU NEED TO LEAVE

Her split lip still stung. At least she was dry again and somewhat clean.

Too fearful to strip and shower, Megan had filled the sink with warm, soapy water, and with her body pressed against the bolted door, she had wiped herself clean as best she could. She had slipped into fresh, dry clothes and wrapped up her wet, muddy ones. She soaked a fresh cloth in cold water and wrung it out before scurrying back to the guest room. *Her room*, she realised she had come to think of it. And in such a short space of time.

Now she sat on the edge of the iron bed, her nerves as wrought as her muscles, dabbing the cold cloth against her stinging mouth.

Ted lay on the carpet by her feet, his furry brown body warming her frozen toes.

The dog was sitting patiently outside the bathroom door when she opened it, and he hadn't left her side since. The dog had shown more loyalty and affection towards her than any human being within this house. A sad state of affairs for sure.

Megan leaned forward and tousled his soft ears. Dogs were such pure creatures. They offered everything of themselves to their people, never asking anything in return. For some, they were just a blip on the radar of their life, a pet they had as a child or a pet they had gifted their own child. But to each dog, that person was the sum of their entire short life. The thought made her forlorn, and she pushed it from her mind.

Not her dog. Not her problem.

And Finn clearly cared a great deal for the animal, even if nobody else much acknowledged its existence.

Ted gazed up at her, his tongue lolling contentedly from his mouth. Like he knew she was thinking about him specifically.

Something clattered against the window outside.

Her breath caught in her throat, and Megan sat still as a stone, waiting to see what would happen next.

A bird? Michael playing tricks on her?

The minutes ticked by, but the sound did not repeat.

Standing slowly, Megan moved with trepidation towards the curtains that covered the glass.

With a slow count beneath her breath . . . one . . . two . . . three . . . she grasped the drapes and whisked them back.

And screamed as a broad hand slapped the window again, fingers splayed against the glass.

Megan stumbled away, attempting to create distance between her and the figure in the yellow raincoat.

Liam O'Keefe slapped the window again, but lighter this time, and despite her quaking fear, Megan halted and turned back to face him. The rain had begun to fall in sheets again, and the man cut a lonely figure. Water coursed down, the tiny rivers turning to rivulets as they met his splayed fingers and were forced to change course. Lightening flashed, turning the yard beyond the window into a comic book strip of monochrome shades. The jagged scar that ran across Liam's face seemed to glow in the ethereal light. He opened his mouth to speak but a sudden burst of thunder muffled words that were already dulled by the sheet of glass that separated them.

Megan's heart fluttered in her chest. She gazed at the figure beyond the window and saw nothing to fear. The man who had scared her so frequently in such a short span of time smiled sadly at her.

"You need to get away from here," he shouted, his words barely audible through the watery deluge. "You need to leave. NOW!"

Another thunderous crack ripped the night apart. A misty scarlet spray covered the glass, blocking Liam from her view, and before she knew what she was doing, Megan found herself pressed against the window.

Through the stained window, Liam swayed on his feet. He was facing away from her, watching intently as a shape approached him in the darkness. Another bolt of lightning lit up the scene and Megan gasped.

Denny slunk towards them, a shotgun braced against his shoulder. Shay followed close behind.

Liam turned back towards Megan and with horror, she realised half his face was missing. The red mist suddenly made more sense and tears filled her eyes as she gaped at the gristly mess of the older man's ruined face.

One side of his mouth lifted again, the ghost of a smile on his broken visage, as he mouthed one word. Another shot rang out, and Megan screamed as the rest of Liam's head disappeared in a splatter of blood and bone. Her ears rang, a shrill buzzing dominating her senses, but she knew she was still screaming. She could hear herself as though from a distance. The only thing penetrating the static buzzing in her head was the image of Liam's mouth moving as he mimed that final word at her, his remaining eye filled with so much sadness but still a modicum of hope. She knew what he had said.

Run.

Before she could stop and talk herself out of it, Megan turned to do exactly that. To run. But to her horror, a dark form filled the doorway, arms reaching out for her.

She screamed once more.

20. WHAT THE FUCK IS GOING ON HERE?

"It's me, Megan. It's only me."

As Finn reached out for her, Megan collapsed to the floor, her body wracked with shuddering sobs. "They killed him, Finn! They shot him!" Her voice rose as she spoke, and as the scene replayed in her mind, she grew more hysterical. Alongside her panic and fear, anger began to sprout in her stomach, writhing and hot. She lifted her eyes to Finn, her gaze hard. "What the fuck is going on here?"

"I don't know what you think you saw, but I promise you, we can get it all straightened out. You need to calm down first," he said, his voice urgent.

Pulling herself from the floor, Megan moved away from Finn and sat on the bed. Her eyes shot daggers in his direction, but she willed herself to calm down. Swallowing her anger, she said, "I know what I just witnessed. Your family just shot that O'Keefe man in the face, Finn. In the *fucking* face!" Finn crossed the room cautiously, his hands out before him in a placating manner as though approaching a wild animal. He sat next to her on the bed but left space between them. Whether for his benefit or hers, Megan wasn't sure.

HUSH, MY DARLING

"Okay, I know how bad this looks, but listen to me for a minute, please. That man has haunted my family for years. *Years.* You said yourself that he scared you when you first met him. He wanted you to go with him. Do you really believe you would have been safe with someone who not only stood in front of your car but tried to get into the car after you? You were terrified when me and Da found you. You were locked in the car, for fuck's sake! He's been skulking around the woods around our property. He was at your window! Why was he at your window, Megan?"

Faltering, she looked at her feet. "I don't know. He was warning me. About your family. About you. He told me I needed to run." Finally, she lifted her eyes to meet his and flinched as he stared at her, visibly hurt.

"We took you in. We gave you a bed and food and anything else you've needed. My brother is trying to fix your car. You should be thanking him. He probably just saved your life." Finn stood and turned to leave. Megan caught his arm, stopping him in his tracks.

"You're right," she said. "I'm sorry. I really am grateful, but so much weird stuff has happened. Your family is hard to judge. I'm pretty sure Shay and Denny hate me. Ma too. Someone has been messing with me, taking my stuff. My phone is still missing. I was already on edge, and I literally just watched a man's face being blown off!" She knew she was getting hysterical again, and before she could stop them, the tears started to fall free and hot from her eyes. "This is all too much, Finn," she sobbed.

Dropping to his knees on the carpet, he pulled her into his arms. Megan sobbed, unable to contain the emotions battling inside her.

Finn held her quietly, his hands strong and pressing heavily against her shoulder blades until, eventually, the sobs subsided to watery hiccups. Megan pulled away, embarrassed at her emotional outburst, but Finn just smiled kindly.

"You're right, my darling," he said. "You've been through a lot the past few days. And I know the family are an odd bunch. Denny had no right to lay a hand on you earlier, but you need to understand: he's an old-fashioned man being raised by an even older old-fashioned man. He's a prick, especially to women, but he doesn't even realise it. I promise he doesn't hate you. In fact, it's probably the opposite since he's so gruff with you. Probably has his eye on you."

Megan's mouth dropped, horrified at the prospect, and Finn burst into laughter.

"Don't worry," he said as he moved towards the door. "He wouldn't dare make a move on you when he knows I have eyes for you too. You need a drink after that shock. Hang on and I'll grab us something strong!"

Without waiting for a response, he was gone, his footsteps echoing away down the corridor.

He wouldn't dare make a move on you when he knows I have eyes for you too.

Despite everything that had happened, Megan found a warmth blooming in her stomach, one completely different than the myriad of emotions she'd felt over the past hour. Finn was probably right. The O'Keefe man had been behaving oddly from the outset. Still, it sickened her every time she pictured his ruined face. Nobody deserved to die like that. She was shocked by the lengths they had gone to.

Shooting a man seemed extreme and she had never witnessed a violent incident like it in her life, but she had heard stories of people shooting trespassers on their land. Plus, Dominic Brogan was police. She was sure they had probably already contacted him to get the whole thing straightened out. Megan pulled herself further onto the bed, wiggling until her back hit the intricate iron headboard, then pulled her knees up to her stomach.

With a small smile, she listened intently for Finn's return. Still, her eyes didn't return to the window. She didn't want to look. Couldn't.

And then the ghostly crying began again, drifting up through the vent like some kind of melancholy music.

21. My Teddy Bear

"Do you hear it?" Megan hissed, grabbing Finn's arm as he re-entered the room. "The crying. I told you I really heard something!"

Wrinkling his face, Finn moved closer to the vent where the muffled sobbing travelled from. Placing two glasses and the bottle he held onto the dresser, Finn lowered himself to the carpet with a soft grunt. Megan opened her mouth to speak again, but he silenced her with a solitary finger in the air. The crying faded away to nothing, and he rocked back on his heels and looked at her with bemusement.

"'Tis only them old vents. They run through the basement. Probably displaced air with that storm." He stood and brushed his knees, then grabbed a glass and held it out to her. "Nothing will calm the nerves like a drop of whiskey. This will help too." In his palm he held half a pill, its broken jagged centre leaving a chalky trail on his hand. "They're very mild sedatives. Perfectly safe and exactly what you need after all that excitement."

With a raised eyebrow, Megan took the proffered glass and watched as he filled it with the amber liquid. "I don't think that's the word I'd use to describe it." Still, she scooped the pill from his hand and tossed it into her mouth, chasing it down with a deep swig of whiskey.

With a chuckle, Finn filled his own, set the bottle back on the dresser, and clinked his glass against hers.

"Sláinte!" He tossed it back and quickly refilled his glass. Crossing the room, Finn dropped onto the bed and scooted backwards until his spine was against the wall.

Megan followed shyly and settled herself at the head of the bed.

"Throw us a pillow there," said Finn, reaching an arm out.

With a giggle, Megan pulled one of the two pillows from behind her and tossed it at him.

"Hey!" he yelled, nearly spilling his drink as he grabbed the pillow before it could hit him full force. They both laughed, and any tension that had lingered in the room dissipated.

They talked more. Conversation came easily between them, and Megan found herself opening up once more about her troubled family life back home.

As she dissected her relationship with her mother, the begrudgery she felt towards her half-sister, and her hatred for Eric that still burned bright and hot all these years later, she was horrified to realise that tears were threatening to spill over again.

Finn, somehow recognising her distress, expertly steered the conversation to her father. He listened with delight as she told him about the hours they had spent in the forest when she was a girl.

"It all started because I almost ate a death cap mushroom." She laughed, the memory still so clear in her mind. "Dad almost had a heart attack! From then on, he took me out at every opportunity to teach me about the different things the forest had to offer. He taught me what was safe to eat and what could kill me. He even taught me some of the medicinal properties. It was the best time of my life."

"Well, I'm glad he saved you from the poison mushroom! If he were around, I'd shake the man's hand," Finn said with a smile. "Why did you stop?"

Megan looked at him.

"How do you know we stopped?" she asked.

"Your face. You got this wistful look towards the end. Tells me you wish you had experienced it some more."

"How very astute of you, Mr Brogan," she smirked, then exhaled a long sigh. "Life just got in the way. Dad had to work longer hours to keep things afloat on his own. Then my teenage years rolled around, and well, you know how it is. Everything is more interesting than being in the woods with your old man. I'd give anything to get that time back now, though."

Finn reached out and touched her hand, a small gesture but one that meant a lot in that moment. Without thinking, Megan opened her fingers and laced them through his. It felt right. It felt like she should have done it the moment they met.

He watched her, his gaze intense, but she couldn't quite read the expression on his face. There was still so much mystery about him, and rather than scare her, it gave her a frisson of excitement.

The bedroom door opened, and Ted padded in. His tail went into overdrive when he saw his two favourite people settled on the bed before him. He leapt up, pressing his body against one and then the other until they lost their grip on each other and gave in to his doggy demands. Megan cooed and scratched his ears as he stared at her with doleful brown eyes. Finn gave the dog a hearty scratch before hopping off the bed. He strode across the room and grabbed the bottle by the neck before sauntering back to the bed. Ted had taken up residence by Megan's knees, and Finn grinned and rolled his eyes as he moved to the only available space further down the bed.

As soon as Finn made himself comfortable, the dog launched itself at him, his tail a blur of motion as he assaulted his owner with sloppy kisses. Finn laughed and wrestled the dog. Ted rolled around enthusiastically and barked as Finn gave up, holding his hands out in a gesture of surrender. Megan watched their antics with amusement.

"You really do love him, don't you?" She reached out to ruffle the dog's ears. Ted grunted and flopped back against her, all thoughts of wrestling forgotten in exchange for comfort.

"How could anyone not love him? He's a big eejit, but he's my big eejit. I've had him since he was only a pup. Teddy Bear has been with me through a lot."

"Teddy Bear?" Megan raised an eyebrow at him.

"Yep," Finn said, deadpan. "I'm an easy-going man, but if anyone touches my Teddy Bear, there'll be trouble. You can tease me all you want, but I think you're just jealous that you don't have your own Teddy Bear."

"Touché," she replied, a soft smile playing on her lips as she stroked the sleeping dog's soft fur. There was something comforting about him.

"So, animals are really your jam, then?" she asked, looking across at Finn.

He sipped his drink and nodded.

"How did you become a vet?" she asked. "Like, was there a lot of work involved?"

Finn adjusted his position to something more comfortable.

"I'm actually not a qualified vet," he said sheepishly. "That's not how we roll around here. Denny had an interest in cars as a kid, so Da and Dom taught him everything they knew. He started an apprenticeship with a mechanic in town, but it was a hassle to get in and out, so once he had learned enough, he just continued on by himself. He's smart, so a lot of what he knows is self-taught. It's much the same for me."

Megan looked at him incredulously. "You taught yourself how to be a vet?" she asked, her face horrified.

Finn laughed. "You can wipe that look off your face, girly. I didn't grow up experimenting on animals or running weird trials in the barn like some kind of Dr Frankenstein. I've always loved animals. Loved helping with the pigs and the chickens. We even had a few horses back in the day, but there was no real benefit to us having them, so they ended up being sold. There was a local man at the time who happened to be a vet, which was handy for Da because it meant he had someone close by if anything went wrong. It was cheaper too. They had some kind of arrangement worked out, although God knows what it was. Da would deal with the Devil himself if there was something good in it for him." Finn chuckled. "Mr Byrne, the vet, took me under his wing and started bringing me around with him. He taught me everything he knew. He ended up moving to Australia with the wife to be nearer their daughter and grandkids who had emigrated out there a few years earlier. The farmers in the area call on my services when they need me. They know I'm not properly qualified, but I'm damn good with animals. They pay me, happy that I'm local and cheaper than a real vet. I'm happy to have money in my pocket for doing something I love."

Megan watched his face as he spoke. His eyes lit up as he talked, and his hands became animated. The passion he had for his trade was evident, regardless of how legitimate his qualifications were. Heat rose inside her, and Megan couldn't decide if it was from the whiskey or from the man who sat on the other side of the bed. And now he was beside her. He had moved closer without her even realising.

Before she could think about it anymore, she leaned forward, silencing him with a kiss.

It was tender and gentle, but there was so much more behind it.

They could both feel it.

Pulling away from him, she eyed Finn carefully as she tried to gauge his reaction. Had she made a mistake? They stared at each other for a moment before coming together again.

This time, it was different.

It was fire and passion, longing and wanting, as they threw themselves together in a tangle of limbs.

As she tried to pull her T-shirt over her head, Megan lost her balance and hit the ground with a thump. She burst into peals of laughter, and Ted yelped, jumping from the bed and running from the room at the sudden intrusion to his sleep. Finn stood and reached for her, pulling her off the floor and back into his arms. He walked her backwards towards the open door, his mouth on her temples, her jaw, her lips, her neck. Without breaking from her, he reached an arm behind her and pushed the door. It closed heavily, and for a moment, Megan's cheeks flamed at the prospect of the rest of the household figuring out exactly what was going on. But as Finn's mouth moved lower, his hands lower again, all thoughts of the extended Brogan clan left her mind in a puff of smoke.

Her mind empty and her body on fire, Megan pulled Finn down, the two of them tumbling onto the iron bed. As they melded together, panting and gasping, bodies writhing, the only sound beyond their union was that of the relentless rain still drumming down outside.

22. A Happy Ending

*C*RACK!

Bolting upright in the bed, Megan flailed around in the darkness. Beyond the window, the sky lit up again as the storm continued to rage. The weather grew angrier with each passing moment. Slowly, as sleep washed away from her and her senses returned, Megan's panicked heart began to calm. The ice that had fused in her veins was replaced by warmth as memories of Finn flooded in. Settling back down, she reached out for him.

The space he had occupied was empty and cold.

Megan sat upright again and rubbed at her eyes. The room slowly swam back into something approaching focus. The longer she looked, the more substantiated the dark shapes in the room became. The dresser, the lamp, the suitcase on the floor, all black shapes, but a deeper black in the murky gloom. Her eyes flicked towards the door.

It was closed tight in its frame, the tiniest hint of light just barely visible beneath the crack at the bottom.

With a sigh, Megan dropped back against the pillows and willed herself back to sleep.

The memory of Finn's body moving as one with her own played like a reel in her head and lit her nerve endings on fire, and she groaned, annoyed with herself for obsessing about him. She tossed and turned until darkness finally took her graciously into its depths once more.

***

With a jolt, Megan woke, her troubled dreams sloughing from her like dead flesh.

The gloom beyond the window had lightened some. Morning was here.

Someone knocked on the bedroom door, gently at first, then heavier.

"Who is it?" she called softly.

Without any reply, the door swung open, and Dominic stepped into the room. Megan eyed him suspiciously.

"Morning, Miss Megan," he said cheerfully, ignoring the look on her face and making no apology for the intrusion. "Just wanted to check in with you while I'm here and see how you're holding up after last night."

"You mean after watching a man get his head blown off?" she asked, sarcasm dripping from her tone like poison.

"Yes," he said simply.

The two stared at one another until Megan folded beneath the large man's intense gaze and dropped her eyes.

"I'm not doing great, to be honest, Dominic," she said. "Do I need to give a statement or anything like that?"

"Nothing like that, my darling," he said, his gaze holding steady. "I've taken care of everything. You don't have to worry about Mr O'Keefe anymore. He can't hurt you now."

Megan's head whipped upwards. She stared incredulously at Dominic and laughed, though there was no humour in it.

"I'm not worried about him. I don't think he ever wanted to hurt me to begin with," she said.

"Now, believe me, girl, that man was a threat. You should be out there on your hands and knees thanking Denny and Shay for taking care of that nasty business. What kind of man skulks around someone's private property peeping in windows at young women? Huh? The world is better off without the likes of him. Fucking busybody."

The callous way he spat the words out startled Megan, and she groaned inwardly as she felt tears build – a well of emotion suddenly swelling up inside her. She willed herself not to cry in front of Dominic, but it was too late. Fat tears rolled down her face and plopped onto the blanket that swaddled her, tiny wet patches spreading like a pox around her.

"There, there, my lovely. I know it's a lot to take in," he said as he moved towards her.

Despite her best efforts, she flinched at his approach and knew by the tilt of his head that it hadn't gone unnoticed.

With a shrug, he turned back towards the dresser where the almost empty whiskey bottle sat. Plucking one of the glasses from where it rested, he bustled out of the room, and Megan heard water gush from the bathroom tap. The water silenced and Dominic bustled back into the room. He emptied the bottle into the glass and strode across the room, depositing the drink in her hand.

"Drink," he said. "It will settle those emotions."

And despite her better judgement and the fact that it was early morning, she did as she was told.

Tossing the glass back, she swallowed the whiskey, gulping it down her throat. She hissed as the fiery warmth spread through her body, and it *did* calm her nerves.

Dominic sat on the edge of the bed and watched her, studying her face. Then he reached out and touched her cheek tenderly, wiping away a solitary tear that failed to catch up with the others as they had rolled away. Megan flinched again as his cold fingers glanced her skin.

With a wry smile, he pulled his hand away, letting it drop onto the blanket near her own.

"See?" he said softly. "Didn't I tell you that would make you feel better? You've had a tough night, haven't you, sweetheart?"

Megan nodded.

Her head felt like a lead weight on her shoulders.

She cursed herself for gulping down the whiskey. She wasn't a huge drinker to begin with, and she could feel it go straight to her head.

"Although, from what I hear, the night didn't end terribly for you. I heard it had a happy ending." Dominic chuckled.

Alarm bells tried to sound in Megan's head, but her mind was thick and swimming, like a fog of molasses had filled the space behind her eyes. Her fingers and toes tingled, and her skin buzzed like a thousand insects were marching across her body in waves.

Something was wrong.

She wasn't a big drinker, but the effect that one drink had on her was too much. Tentacles of unease unfurled in her stomach as the edges of her vision softened and blurred. And then Dominic was right in front of her. The only thing she could see as his head grew larger. His mouth pressed against hers. Her stomach roiled as the sour taste of him permeated her daze just enough. Megan pushed him away and spat at him.

"Don't you fucking touch me!" she tried to yell, but it escaped her mouth as a whisper. Panic crawled along her skin like an army of tiny spiders. Her body was failing her.

Dominic grabbed Megan's hands and trapped them behind her head, pushing himself closer to her until he lay across her, his body so heavy it squeezed the breath from her lungs.

"Don't think for a second that Finn is the only one getting all the fun around here," he hissed. His mouth moved from her ear to her neck as he planted slobbery, wet kisses on her skin.

Time felt as though it had frozen, and Megan knew if she didn't act now, she was going to pass out from whatever Dominic had put in her drink. Because he must have put something in it. If she passed out, she knew what would happen. Pinpricks of black spotted her vision, and her senses were filled with the stench of sweat and excitement that rolled off the large man.

She took a breath, sucking the stagnant air deep into her lungs.

Megan screamed.

Her scream cut off as Dominic backhanded her. She could taste blood in her mouth, and stars spotted her vision now alongside the pinpricks of black. That was it. Her only chance. And if anybody heard, would they even care?

23. THE LABRADOR OR THE BITCH?

Something moved down the hall like lightning, four paws hitting the floor rapidly like a burst of gunfire. The bedroom door burst open, and Ted raced into the room. The dog snarled and lunged at Dominic, its teeth gnashing.

With a roar of pain, he shuffled off her immobile frame, and as the breath poured back into her squashed lungs, Megan offered up a silent prayer to any deity that cared to listen. With great effort, she dragged herself upright. Her eyelids fluttered sporadically as she fought to hold off the effects of whatever sedative coursed through her system. Tears fell again as she watched the dog hurl itself at Dominic, its teeth still bared.

The commotion must have finally drawn someone's attention because footsteps moved urgently through the house. Dominic shouted and swore as he attempted to keep Ted at bay.

As the dog lunged again, Dominic was ready and lashed out with a heavy kick.

With a yelp, Ted fell to the floor. Before the dog could recover, Dominic loomed over the animal and drove another kick into its side.

Megan cried out in tandem with Ted and rolled her heavy bones to the floor. She crashed to the ground and tried to pull herself across the carpet. The dog had saved her life. She needed to save his.

Before she could make much progress, Finn burst into the room. His mouth was set in a grim line, and he glanced briefly at Megan on the floor before turning his attention to Ted.

He shoved Dominic away from the dog roughly.

"Get the fuck away from my dog," he growled.

Dominic stood and crowed with laughter. "Which dog would that be? The Labrador or the bitch?" He nodded his head from Ted to Megan as he spoke, a spiteful glee on his face. "You think you get to have all the fun around here, Finn? It's been too fucking long since we've got one this easily and you think you can just claim her? Respect your fucking elders, boy!"

The two men launched at each other, arms swinging and fists flying.

A cacophony of voices filled the room from every angle, and through heavy eyes, Megan watched from the floor as more feet appeared at the door and the two men were pulled apart. She couldn't fight it any longer. Her eyes drifted closed and the world ceased to exist.

24. A WHOLE SHITSTORM OF BAD

The window was boarded over from the outside, just a hint of light leaking through small gaps in the hastily erected boards.

Megan screamed, a white-hot rage coursing through her veins. She hit the glass hard, but it hurt her hand more than the window.

Not even a crack.

She knew if the boards weren't there blocking her way, she wouldn't have thought twice about throwing something through it. The lamp. A drawer from the dresser. She wouldn't have stopped until she had gained her freedom.

They clearly weren't taking any chances.

All of the niggling doubts she had throughout her short stay culminated in the ultimate slap in the face.

When she'd come to, Megan found herself alone on the little iron bed. Her whole body ached, and her lip was swollen and stinging from the double assault. First Denny had hit her, then Dominic. Her stomach had twisted and turned at the memory of the large man's body pressed against her own, his hands as they wandered around her body, touching her in places she hadn't wanted to be touched. A haze hung from her like a cobweb, a holdover from whatever Dominic had spiked her drink with. Stumbling to the door, the first threads of panic bloomed when the handle wouldn't turn.

She jiggled and pulled, but the door hadn't budged.

Blind panic replaced any remaining sluggishness, and Megan screamed and shouted and threw herself at the door repeatedly until she feared injury. Rubbing her aching shoulder, knowing that bruises were probably already blooming on her skin, she rushed to the window and drew back the curtains, then sank to the floor as the full force of reality crashed down upon her.

The window was boarded.

The door was locked.

There was no escape.

She stayed puddled on the carpet, her face wet with tears. All the red flags she had missed or chosen to overlook nipped at her subconscious now like mosquitos on a hot day. She allowed herself those moments of grief.

And that was what she felt.

Grief.

Megan had a strong feeling that she would die in this house.

The irony of her first encounter with Finn and Shay wasn't lost on her. That fear she had felt as Finn approached, axe in one hand, rope in the other. And then she saw his pretty face and that was all it took for her to overlook everything that had happened since.

Stupid.

Stupid.

STUPID!

She needed to calm down and figure this out. If she gave up hope now, she was all but signing her own death warrant.

Pulling in deep through her nostrils, the musty air of the entombed bedroom filling her lungs, she released each breath, allowing the air to hiss slowly through her teeth. Squeezing her eyes shut, Megan ran her fingers over the carpet. Tiny pieces of grit and dirt rubbed along her fingertips, and she allowed each sensation to ground her.

Through the vent to her left, a soft voice carried on the air, and Megan's eyes snapped open. The words were muffled and hard to decipher, but she had no doubt that it was the same girl.

The crying girl.

Rising to her knees and shuffling along the carpet, Megan pressed her ear to the vent and listened.

The words continued, interspersed with soft crying.

"Hey," Megan whispered into the vent. "Can you hear me?"

The girl continued speaking in muffled bursts, but there was no indication that she had heard Megan.

And then it hit her.

Rising quickly, Megan stumbled across the small room to the iron bed and reached for the pillow. She pushed her hand into the pillowcase and fumbled around until her fingers brushed metal. Pulling the chain out, the silver letters glinting in the dull light, she looked from the delicate piece of jewellery to the vent.

Throwing herself back across the room and onto the floor by the vent, she spoke again, louder this time, "Lauren? Can you hear me?"

The garbled speech fell silent, and Megan's heart swelled. She had an ally. Someone to help figure a way out of this wretched place!

But the silence continued, and with a sinking feeling in her gut, Megan knew that Lauren hadn't heard her. She closed her fingers around the chain, squeezing it tight until the sharp edges of the letters bit into her skin.

Footsteps sounded in the corridor outside, and as they drew closer, Megan moved quickly. Someone came to a stop outside the door and moving quietly into place on the bed, she repositioned herself and slid the chain back into the pillowcase. She snatched her hand back and rested it casually on her lap just as the door swung inward.

Finn stepped in, closing the door behind him. He looked sheepishly at her before approaching. Megan watched him guardedly, then turned her head away as he sat beside her.

"How are ya feeling?" he asked gently, reaching for her hand.

Snatching her hand away, Megan rounded on him, her anger spilling over in hot bursts. "How the fuck do you think I feel, Finn? Your whole fucking family has been gaslighting me since I got here. Your brother hit me. Your uncle tried to fucking *rape* me! I'm locked in this room like a prisoner. Did you know the window is boarded up outside? Who the fuck does that?"

He looked at her impassively, the muscles in his jaw twitching.

"I know you're angry, darling. Don't look at it as being a prisoner; see it as me trying to keep you safe. It could be worse. If I hadn't claimed you, they'd all be tearing you apart now like a bunch of wild animals. It's been a long time since a new girl has landed on our doorstep. Believe me, Dominic and Denny, especially Denny, would like nothing better than to drag you downstairs and do . . . well, all kinds of horrible things to you. Frankly, you should be happy that you're mine. I think we could have something really special, Megan. I know you don't see it that way right now. You're angry, I get it. But you will see it. We can be happy."

Megan stared at him, the earnest look on his face souring her stomach. Finn smiled at her. It was the kind of smile that would have made her stomach flip just twenty-four hours ago, but now, she fought to quell the queasiness crawling up her throat.

"Claimed me?" she whispered in disbelief. "You're as fucking crazy as the rest of your goddamned fucking family! That man, Liam O'Keefe, he really was trying to warn me! If I had just gone with him after the crash, I'd be safe. Oh my God. What have I done?" The full weight of her decisions bore down on Megan like boulders, and tears sprung from her eyes once more. "You killed him. Blew his fucking head off, and all he tried to do was save me. From you! I'm not yours, Finn. I'll never be yours," she spat, lunging towards him. Stars exploded behind her eyes, and suddenly Megan was on the floor looking up. Finn towered over her, his jaw tight and his dark eyes flashing with rage. His arm hung loosely by his side. His hand was still bunched into the fist that had floored her.

"Don't test me, Megan. Things can go really well for you. Or they can go really fucking bad. I have to go help the others clear the yard after the storm. I'll check back in a bit with some dinner. I hope you're in better form then."

He stepped across her and stalked from the room, the door banging in the frame behind him. The key rattled in the lock, and his footsteps receded as he walked away.

Megan stood shakily.

This was bad. This was a whole shitstorm of bad. She needed to figure out how to get out of here and away from the Brogan clan.

And she needed to figure it out fast.

25. FUCK THIS HOUSE

Megan had formulated a plan.

As she lay on the bed, her body aching and her mind fractured, thoughts of her dad overwhelmed her. He had ended his life to save her from the pain of watching him die a slow and agonising death. And how did she repay his sacrifice? By winding up in the situation she was in, facing down a slow and agonising death of her own.

A prisoner.

As her mind replayed scenes from her life, images of her dad were overlapped by flashes of her being subjected to all manners of degrading and horrible things at the hands of the monsters who held her captive. All of it played out in her head like an old reel of film, the real and the nightmare, all spliced together like a bad home movie.

She saw herself walking through the forest back home, hand in hand with her dad as he stopped to point at different flowers or explain the differences between death cap and puffball mushrooms. She saw herself tied to the little iron bed, her body being brutalised by a band of leering faces that floated above her. She saw her dad reading her favourite scary stories to her before bed, then running to her side in the dead of night to soothe the frantic nightmares he had forewarned her of. She saw herself withering away as the days passed slowly in this hellhole. She saw the pride in her dad's face the first time she successfully unlocked a door using only a straightened piece of wire during one of his more unusual life skills lessons. She saw herself, a beaten and bloodied shadow of who she once was. She saw the empty pill bottles scattered on the sheet. She saw.

She saw.

She saw a way out.

Megan bolted upright in bed and rummaged in the pillowcase once more for the chain. Her fingers glanced across the metal, tracing each letter of the name.

Lauren.

Her face a mask of determination, she pulled and twisted at the metal. The loops started to unfurl quicker than she had expected, and with a sense of exhilaration, she worked faster. Megan could practically smell the freedom.

She needed to get out the front door and across the front yard. Once she made it to the winding laneway that led away from the house, she'd have a little breathing room. She'd need to be careful not to overexert herself because she still had no idea where she was. She was as lost now as she had been on the mountain road the night she crashed.

But she knew now that there were other houses around. Other *people*. People who traded with the Brogans. People who used Finn's veterinary skills and Denny's mechanical abilities. People who knew the Brogans as good neighbours, but potentially people who knew who they really were beneath the surface.

Just like the O'Keefe family had.

She could find one person willing to help and call the guards. She'd have to be very careful about not alerting Dominic. These were all minor things right now, though. Now, her focus needed to be on straightening the metal letters of the chain enough to unlock the bedroom door.

From the vent, the pitiful crying started again. This time, it fuelled Megan's determination. She would get out of here. She would rescue herself and Lauren too.

Fuck this house. And fuck the Brogans.

Every last one of them.

Satisfied that she had enough of a point to work with, Megan approached the door quietly. Pressing an ear to its surface, she listened.

Nothing.

It seemed like the coast was clear. Hopefully the storm had caused enough damage to require all hands on deck outside. Sure, Ma was probably still in the house somewhere, but she knew she could easily best the frail old woman if she tried to stand between Megan and her freedom.

Slipping the metal strand into the keyhole, Megan moved it around as gently as she could, familiarising herself with the mechanics of the lock. The longer it took, the more her stress levels rose, and Megan knew she needed to stop and take a breath before she ended up damaging the only lifeline she had. If the metal broke, her chance at freedom was gone.

She stilled her hand and took a few deep breaths, her ears constantly straining for any noise within the house. And then she tried again, wiggling the metal into place and jimmying it around until . . . *click*.

Excitement bubbled up inside her, threatening to overwhelm her. It seemed stupid to be so happy, but then, she supposed, she had never had her freedom threatened as absolutely as it had been today. Desperation could turn the tiniest win into a celebration. She needed to keep a clear head, though. The lock was the easy part.

Now she needed to make it through the house and out the door to freedom.

Megan counted to three, pulled the door open as quietly as she could, and slipped out into the hallway.

26. Taste the Freedom

Moving silently through the gloomy corridor, Megan strained her ears for any sounds. The house was quiet.

Too quiet.

The silence was oppressive, and it set her teeth on edge as she moved, one small step at a time, through the hallway. When she reached the corner, all the breath left her body. She knew the front door loomed. It was right there, and yet, it felt a million miles away. The only thing that stood between her and freedom was a straight stretch of dingy carpet, but it felt like a gauntlet, a marathon. How quickly the fear had settled into her bones as seamlessly as a cancer wasn't lost on her. It fuelled her anger. She could almost taste the freedom.

Megan peered around, the adrenaline surging through her.

A shadow moved in the small, frosted glass square set high in the front door.

Someone was coming.

Whipping her head out of view, she glanced around, frustration and fear warring inside her. No way was she going back to her room. Her prison.

Around the corner, someone pushed the front door open and in a blind panic, Megan reached for the closest handle and pushed open the door nearest to her.

Slipping inside, she pulled the door over. If she closed it properly, the sound could alert whoever had entered. She didn't know where they were. They could have detoured into the kitchen. They could be right around the corner.

It wasn't a chance she was willing to take, so Megan stood in the darkness, one eye watching through the open crack. A voice travelled along the hallway, and she prepared for whoever was coming towards her. Denny moved past the door.

And stopped dead in his tracks.

Megan moved a little deeper into the shadows. She held her breath, heart hammering in her chest, and waited.

After a moment, Denny moved on. The basement door opened with a heavy thud, and his boots clattered down the wooden steps. Megan released a shaky breath and pressed a hand against her chest, willing her heart to settle. Her thoughts instantly jumped to Lauren, trapped in the basement. She needed to get out. She needed to get help.

Slowly, silently, she pulled the door open again, preparing to make a burst for the front door and her freedom. She counted down . . . three . . . two . . .

Hands grabbed her from behind, gripping her around the waist. Tears sprang to her eyes as she tried to twist her head around in the darkness. One hand moved from her waist to cover her mouth as she was hoisted backwards.

She wouldn't have screamed anyway.

To scream was to sign her own death warrant.

27. JUST a BOY

Falling to the bed with a grunt, Megan barely had a second to gather her senses when a weight landed on top of her. Rancid breath invaded her nostrils and the hand not covering her mouth moved along her body. She yelped as fingers pinched and plucked at her T-shirt. The fingers slid beneath the thin material and her stomach flipped as they crawled along her skin like spiders, higher and higher, tugging at her bra as they tried to gain entry.

She wouldn't scream.

She slapped and fought but the weight bore down on her, and the more she tried to wriggle out from beneath them, the more excited the form became. The darkness held just as much weight as the body on top of her. As she drew her arm back again to launch another attempted assault on her assailant, Megan hit something hard. A lamp.

She stretched beneath the figure, moaning in horror as they began to grind their hips hard against her. Fumbling her hand at the lamp and slapping around its base, she quickly found a switch and clicked it on.

Grandpa Brogan leered down at her.

Flecks of yellowing spittle mottled the skin around his mouth, and Megan fought to hold in a shriek as the old man moved his head down, aiming his mouth at hers.

She wouldn't scream.

The old man hit his target. His breath was hot and sour against her, and as his tongue darted into her mouth, Megan gagged. Vomit erupted from her churning insides and into Grandpa's mouth. He turned his head and spit the bulk of her ejection from his mouth before turning back towards her, a smile on his wretched face and a glint in his rheumy old eyes.

CRACK!

Megan whacked the old timer with the lamp. He fell to the mattress beside her, holding the side of his face. She had hoped it would do more damage, but the cord hadn't stretched far enough for her to get much velocity behind her swing. Still, she had bought herself an opportunity.

Reaching for the bedside locker, her hands swiping along the junk littered on its surface, she grabbed the closest thing. Beside her, the old man reached out with one hand, grasping at her breast as he tried to find the purchase to heave himself back on top of her. The other hand still cradled his face.

Megan flipped around and stabbed at him, her face stretched in a silent scream. Grandpa fell back with a grunt, his hands fluttering to his neck.

The pen she had grasped from the locker stood erect in the wrinkled skin of his neck. Blood, almost black in the weak lamplight, pooled around the wound and snaked down towards the bedspread in crimson streams.

Before the old man could make any more noise and alert someone to her presence, Megan pulled the pillow from beneath his head and pressed it to his face.

She clambered on top, careful not to wriggle too much lest the dirty, old pervert get any enjoyment from his final moments on this Earth. The thought sickened her, and she pressed the material into his face even more fiercely than before.

"You'll never touch another woman again. Never *hurt* another woman again," she hissed against the pillow. He probably couldn't hear her, but Megan didn't care. It was enough to say the words out loud, however quietly.

Ten minutes passed, and still she sat astride the old man. She knew he was dead, and yet the fear remained that if she moved just a little, he would somehow rise up with that leering, tombstone smile and reach for her.

Footsteps sounded in the hallway outside, and knowing she had no choice now, Megan slipped off Grandpa, leaving the pillow to cover his disgusting face. She didn't want to see it ever again.

As she crept away from the bed and back towards the shadows, the door burst open.

Megan and Michael stared at each other.

She knew he would cry out at any moment and alert the others to her presence beyond the bedroom they had confined her to. In a flash, she was across the room, wrapping an arm around the boy's neck and covering his mouth. Just like his great-grandfather had done to her a short time ago. She didn't want to hurt Michael, though. He was just a boy.

But she couldn't risk him calling out.

"I won't hurt you," she whispered in his ear. "But I am getting the fuck out of this hellhole."

Michael pulled against her suddenly. Summoning everything she had, Megan wrestled the boy back into submission, but it was too late. His eyes widened and he squeaked against her open palm that was splayed across the lower half of his face.

On the bed, blood had begun to seep into the pillow that covered his great-grandfather's face. Michael crumpled against her, and Megan staggered sideways in an attempt to keep them both upright. She cursed herself for the heartache she knew he was experiencing, then cursed herself once more for caring.

As she opened her mouth to speak, a white-hot pain bloomed in her side.

Megan gaped at the bloodspot blooming on her T-shirt, just below her ribs. Before panic could overtake her completely, she let her mind shut down and her body take over. With a jerk, she wrenched the penknife from Michael's hand, tightened her grip on his face to muffle any sound, then arced the weapon around and stabbed him.

As the knife entered his flesh, the panicked gasps he had begun to make were silenced. The air was sucked from the room, and they both stood stock still, like statues carved from the finest marble. Inside her own head, Megan screamed. She was shocked at herself. She supposed Michael was probably shocked, too, but before she could examine her thoughts closely, her body reacted once more.

The instinct to survive had taken over, and Megan both welcomed and lamented it.

The knife came out of Michael's chest with a soft sucking sound. Megan knew that if she made it out of this godforsaken house, she'd never forget that sound as long as she lived. Nor would she forget the muffled whimpering the boy made as she drove the knife into his body again and again.

She stabbed, her arm pulling and arcing in a frenzy until Michael's body became a dead weight and she could no longer hold him up.

With a thud, he hit the floor, and Megan finally saw the full extent of what she had done. The blows she had rained upon him hadn't remained confined to his chest.

Michael's face and neck were a ruin of blood and gore. The knife had sliced and scored almost the entire left side of his upper body, from his eye socket down to his stomach. Choking and gagging, Megan fell to her knees beside his unmoving body. She vomited on the carpet, chunks of sick and strings of bile landing in a steaming pile right next to the ruined face of the teenager.

The teenager she had just stabbed to death.

Megan covered her face with hands slick with blood and cried.

She cried for herself because she never should have been in this position to begin with. Mostly, though, she cried for Michael.

He was innocent at the back of it all. Brought along on this depraved ride purely because of the family he had been born into. It wasn't really his fault.

He was just a boy.

Whatever the Brogan family had planned for her was bad, she knew.

When they discovered that she had killed not one, but two of their family members, their plans would change, and not for the better.

Megan knew that if she didn't escape this house soon, her death would be a long and torturous one. The burning sensation in her side was a stark reminder of it.

Lifting her T-shirt, she winced at the sight of the puncture wound Michael had inflicted on her. It looked worse than it was.

She was no doctor, but Megan could see that the blood had all but slowed to the barest dribble. It hurt, but it wasn't deep, and the visual had hurt a hell of a lot more than the wound itself.

Still, she needed to cover it, at the very least. It wouldn't do to make it worse or leave it open to infection. It crossed her mind briefly that she had no idea what condition the knife had been in to begin with, so infection could already be burning its way through her body, but that was something to worry about later. Right now, she needed to find something to cover it and get the hell out of there.

But what could she use?

Moving quietly to the bedside locker, Megan pulled the top drawer open as gently as she could. She avoided looking at the shape on the bed.

Her first victim.

Shaking the thought from her head, Megan reminded herself that she was the victim here. She wouldn't have hurt anyone if they had just left her alone. The first drawer was a jumble of pill bottles, used tissues – Megan cringed as her fingers brushed against them – and cables. She pulled open the next drawer and zeroed in on a roll of duct tape.

She was sure she had watched a movie once where someone bound their wound with duct tape. Time was running out. It would have to do.

As she plucked the roll from the drawer, her eyes were drawn to the scatter of photos beneath it. All the breath left her body, and time stood still as she lifted the stack out for a closer look. Almost immediately, she tossed them back into the drawer, disgusted at what she saw. As the photos spread out, faces leered at her, frozen in time.

She could see Grandpa Brogan and Shay, both men much younger in appearance. They were naked, as was the woman in the photo. Her face was frozen in a terrified rictus, dirt and blood smeared across it. It was only a photograph, but the fear in her eyes was a living thing. The skin along Megan's spine prickled and she stifled a sob.

Fractured pieces of the other photos showed a variety of women. Each one was different and had varying features, but one thing remained the same.

Their eyes.

Terror, pain, humiliation. Megan could almost feel what they had felt, and she knew this was what awaited her if she was caught.

Closing the drawer softly, she rubbed a stray tear from her face and offered up a silent plea to all those women in the pictures. That they would guide her. Protect her. Get her the fuck out of this house.

Ripping squares from the duct tape roll, she slapped them over her wound and smoothed down the edges. The tape pulled tightly, and each step she took felt as though it was forcing the edges of the wound apart, but at least it couldn't leak any more blood. It was a protection of sorts.

In the hallway, a shout rang out, and with a sinking heart, Megan assumed that her absence had finally been noticed.

They were coming for her.

28. SHE'S GONE

The shadows welcomed her as one of their own as she crept back towards the door.

She listened as boots stomped up the hall. They were coming from the direction of the guest room. Her escape had definitely been noticed.

From her place in the corner, draped in gloom, she watched as Ollie rushed past the door, hollering as he went.

"She's gone! She's not in the room!" he yelled as he raced by, so close that if she had stretched her arm out of the shadows and reached through the open sliver of light, she could have touched him.

The front door banged open, and Ollie's voice faded away as he ran to tell the others of his grim discovery.

The knife!

Megan moved to Michael's body and lifted the knife from the puddle of blood it lay discarded in. With a grimace, she wiped the worst of the dripping gore on the dead boy's sweater and returned to her post by the door. She needed to make a run for it.

Before she could reach for the handle, a door clattered in the hallway and Megan dipped back into the shadows, her heart thudding wildly.

Denny appeared, tugging at his jeans as he stalked past the door. Megan's stomach roiled as her mind flitted to a thousand conclusions of what he had been doing in the basement before his brother had come charging through the house yelling his head off.

Lauren.

With a sinking heart, Megan knew that she couldn't leave this place without her. She knew hopelessness and fear in her short time with the Brogans. She couldn't even begin to imagine what that poor girl had experienced up to this point. And she had no idea that anyone knew of her existence. Megan needed to get to her. Get her away from here.

She needed to save them both.

The front door banged closed, and Megan listened intently.

Nothing.

The house was silent again. She could only hope that they had fanned out around the property looking for her. Or had maybe jumped in the jeep to travel the roads in search of their lost prize. This was the best chance she was going to get.

Easing the door open, she fought against every warring cell in her body that screamed at her to go in the other direction, towards the door. Towards her freedom.

She moved down the hall quickly and pushed the basement door open before she could talk herself out of it. The steps dropped away into the dim space below and with a deep, gulping breath, Megan began to descend.

One foot in front of the other, she moved nimbly down, down, down until she hit the end. A dirt floor stretched out in a long corridor that appeared to bisect the house that stood innocuously above it.

The staircase had emptied her out near one end of the hallway. The only thing to her left was another short set of steps and a pair of steel doors. Megan recalled the cellar doors she had spied outside. The obvious assumption was that those metal doors led further up and out through the cellar entrance. *The easiest way for them to transfer the pig carcasses to whatever room they butchered them in*, Finn had said. Probably easier for them to move their victims around unnoticed too.

Standing at the bottom of the steps, she looked around. There was no point going left. Those doors would be locked, of that she had no doubt. Taking one step to the right, she glanced along the dark hallway. In the dull light, she could see a couple of doors set in the wall further along, directly across from each other. The hallway turned sharply just after those doors. The layout was not dissimilar to the house above but appeared to have fewer doors.

As she approached the first couple of doorways, Megan sang a childhood song in her head to choose which one to try first. She reached for the winner, pushing it open and stepping inside. The room was small and dark, and she fumbled a hand along the wall searching for a switch. As the light flicked on, she gasped.

The small room was filled with suitcases and bags in all shapes, colours, and sizes. The only furniture in the room was a rickety old table shoved into a corner. A large cardboard box sat on the table. Two more boxes were pushed beneath the table's surface. Megan picked her way through the jumble of crap and peered into the box.

Purses, ID cards, driving licenses, jewellery . . . it was a mishmash of personal items. Picking up a small stack of licenses, Megan flicked through them quickly, her stomach dropping as she watched each face fall back into the box.

They were all women.

The last license fell upon the others and Megan forgot to breathe as she stared into the familiar eyes of the woman from the photograph in Grandpa Brogan's bedroom drawer. In the small license picture, her eyes held no fear or pain.

She spun away from the table and stumbled over the cases and handbags. As her knees hit the ground hard, Megan noticed a familiar pattern sticking out of one of the bags.

Her sheep blanket was there, as was the suitcase that had been in the guest room with her. She wracked her brain, trying to recall whether the bag had been there before she escaped. Had they taken it while she was passed out? Before they boarded up the windows? Before they locked her away like a prisoner?

Black spots danced in front of her eyes, and before she could pass out, Megan burst from the room. She closed the door, her body pressing against its cool surface.

On to the next one.

As soon as she opened the second door, she knew what room she was in.

The smell of meat and blood and rot engulfed her, and she bit back a scream as she took in the gore.

Two pig carcasses hung from hooks in the ceiling, their skin stained with bloody rivulets. Metal buckets stood below each pig, slick blood – almost black – collected in each receptacle.

A long countertop ran along one wall, the wood heavily marred and stained from the meat it had held over the years. An arm now lay on the counter's surface, the fingers open as though reaching for something.

Megan turned and vomited.

It wasn't even the dismembered arm that had brought her stomach juices streaming from her mouth.

It was the body that hung just beyond the pig carcasses.

Its legs were tied with heavy rope and strung across another hook that hung down from dirty, rusted chains in the ceiling. There were no clothes covering it, and Megan gagged again as her eyes travelled along the corpse, from its ankles down past its flaccid penis resting against the groin, along the wrinkled skin of its pale stomach, past its neck, and to its head.

29. WHAT A CONVENIENT SNACK

Liam O'Keefe's head was a mess of curls on one side and a mess of gore on the other, the impact of the gunshot clear beneath the harsh fluorescent lights of this abattoir. Since Megan last saw the man, he had lost both arms. She knew where one of them was, and instantly her eyes flicked back to the limb on the countertop. She had no idea where the other one was and had no desire to investigate.

And yet, her eyes scanned along the rest of the counter, coming to rest a little further down where reusable plastic food boxes were stacked. Beside the boxes were the bloody remnants of the other arm, five individual fingers, a bloodied knife, and what looked like a potato peeler.

A small TV sat on the end of the countertop. The images that rolled on the screen were grainy, but there was no disguising the pornographic scenes that played out silently. Another crimson-stained knife and ribbons of skin littered the counter by the television, and next to those was a box of tissues and a dirt-smeared bottle of lubricant. There among the detritus, she noticed a balled-up wad of material: lemon yellow with lavender hearts and stars.

Megan gagged again, tears coursing down her face.

She turned, and in her haste to get out of this hellish room, ran straight into the doorframe. Pain bloomed behind her eye, and her exploratory fingers came away wet with blood. She needed to get a hold of herself. She couldn't afford to pass out or get knocked out down here. If she did, this rescue was as good as done. And if they found her in a crumpled heap in their butchering workshop, well, she didn't want to think about how easy that would make things for them.

What a convenient snack she'd make.

She gagged again, coughing and spluttering as she staggered through the door and back into the dank hallway.

As she rounded the corner, Megan realised she was crying. For a moment, she was glad at the separation between mind and body that was happening to her. She needed to stay strong, even if it was just long enough to find Lauren and get out of this place.

The more distance she put between herself and the abattoir, the more her heart rate settled. She could pretend that none of this was happening, that none of it was real. The reprieve would only be temporary, but it would be enough to get her through the nightmare.

More doors lined the new section of the corridor, but Megan knew in an instant which one she needed to get to.

Right at the end of the hall, a steel door faced her. Hanging from it was a heavy padlock. She wondered idly if they would have eventually put a similar one on the guest room door or if they would have killed Lauren and replaced her down here with Megan.

Fresh meat, and all that.

Picking up the pace, she moved quickly to the door and pressed her ear to its surface. Behind it, soft whimpering was audible, and Megan slapped her hand against the door – gently first, then harder when there was no reaction from within.

"Lauren!" she hissed against the metal. "I'm gonna get you out. I need you to help me, though."

Something banged against the other side of the door, and relief flooded Megan as a voice piped up,

"Who are you? Oh, thank God you're here. Get me the fuck out of here. Please!"

The girl's voice was soft, a quaver evident in her tone. Megan couldn't help but wonder what kind of horrors she had endured down here. The relief that had washed over her faded fast as she tugged uselessly at the padlock. What if Denny had the key in his pocket? Of course he did. She really hadn't thought this thing through, and now she was cornered like an animal if any of the Brogans came down here.

"The keys are usually hanging on the wall by the corner," came the girl's voice, and Megan could have wept as the tightness in her stomach and chest abated just a little.

The light was dull, but she found the keys easily and pulled them from the hook on the wall. Fumbling with the bunch, she tried one after another until, finally, she found one that fit.

A thud echoed through the basement, and Megan froze, her hand shaking against the lock. Afraid to move but desperate to avoid re-capture, she held her breath as she waited and listened. There were no more thuds. The underground space remained silent.

She returned her attention to the door with renewed urgency. The key turned easily, and with a *click*, the padlock popped open and fell to the ground with a heavy, metallic clunk.

Megan pushed the door open. A girl, ragged and dirty, fell through the opening and collapsed into her outstretched arms. Megan held her tightly as the two women leaned into each other and cried. Time was ticking on, and Megan's skin prickled with both elation and terror.

She had freed Lauren, but they still needed to navigate their way out.

Out of the basement.

Out of the house.

Out of this nightmare.

Along the corridor, she tugged the weeping girl behind her, wishing that the other woman would be quiet. Just long enough for them to reach the outside.

After a moment, she pulled back and grabbed the girl's shoulders, forcing Lauren to look into her eyes.

"I'm Megan," she whispered. "I need you to please be quiet. We need to get the fuck out of here." She turned and moved forward, whispering over her shoulder as she rounded the corner, "I found your necklace upstairs. It was clever of you to hide it like that, Lauren."

Lauren pulled at her arm urgently. Megan looked back at her. The girl's dirty blonde hair was stuck to her scalp with grime and knots. Her skin was etched with blood and dirt, as was the thin silk slip that barely covered her trembling body. Megan's heart ached for the broken creature before her.

"What chain?" asked the girl, confusion washing over her delicate features. "I'm not . . ."

An ear-splitting boom drowned out her words.

30. YOU BASTARD

Megan flinched as something wet and hot spattered her face. She turned just in time to see the girl drop heavily to the floor.

Where her pretty, frightened eyes had been was nothing more than a gaping mess of gore. With shaking fingers, Megan wiped her own face. Her hand came away sticky with blood and she stood frozen in shock as a scream gurgled its way up her throat.

Her vision doubled, and she swayed on her feet as she turned back towards the basement stairs. Denny stood in the middle of the hallway, the shotgun in his hands still pointed at the space where the captive girl stood moments ago. When she still had a chance at freedom. When she was still alive.

Almost in response, the body on the floor began to splutter and choke.

Lauren was still alive.

"TILLY!"

A piercing shriek cut through the haze of disbelief that had shrouded Megan. She forced her eyes away from the twitching girl on the floor, casting her eyes back towards the people who stood between her and the outside world.

Denny had lowered the gun. He watched impassively as Ma stumbled down the last few steps. The woman moaned as she looked down the hallway, past Megan, to the mortally wounded girl on the floor.

"You BASTARD!" she screeched, throwing herself at him.

The large man stumbled backwards, and Shay and Ollie appeared at Ma's side and grabbed at her arms. She shook them off as she rounded on Denny again.

He shoved her away hard, and the old woman turned beseeching eyes to her husband.

"You promised," she wailed.

It took her a moment to realise it, but it soon clicked with Megan that whatever was happening between the Brogan family members was big.

Big enough to take their attention off her.

Beyond the squabbling circle, light poured in, casting the short steps to the cellar door in dappled light. Dust motes and dead leaves swirled in the beam, and Megan watched for a moment with detached curiosity.

The cellar door was open.

The door was *open*. Freedom was still within reach.

It was *right there*!

She moved slowly, making herself as small as possible. She passed right behind Denny, so close she could have tried to pull the gun from his grasp.

But that would have been a mistake, and Megan knew it.

Better to continue on . . . slowly . . . undetected.

And then she was at the bottom of the short set of steps. She could taste the wild garlic on the breeze that floated lazily through the open doors. Could hear the gentle cadence of birdsong in the forest that lay just beyond her line of sight.

"GET HER!"

The shout from the hallway spurred her on, and Megan darted up the steps, pulling herself up the incline with her hands.

And then she was outside.

"Megan."

She jolted, turning towards that soft voice.

Finn stood there. His dark eyes held an odd combination of victory and sadness.

Before Megan could react, he swung the bat that she hadn't noticed hanging by his side. It cracked against her skull, and she fell heavily to the dirt as the world closed in around her.

Through heavy eyelids spotted with black, she watched as Finn knelt beside her. He cradled her cheek with a tender touch, and she mewled feebly. Fear and pain overwhelmed her, and the darkness beckoned. Its lure was strong and as she felt Finn gather her gently against his chest and lift her from the dirt, she succumbed to its call, shuddering weakly as he stroked her cheek again and whispered to her, "Hush, my darling."

31. You're No Better Than They Are

Megatron, you need to be less trusting of people. It's gonna get you in trouble someday.

Megan opened her eyes, squinting against the overhead light that felt far too bright. The glare cleaved her skull in two and turned the jackhammer in her head into a thunderous roar.

She blinked and licked her lips.

She couldn't see her dad. Had she only dreamt of him? Or was she dreaming now? Everything felt upside down. She felt as though she had woken from a thousand-year sleep, her mind wrapped in a tight band of mist. Thoughts and memories surfaced, just barely breaching the fog, but she couldn't grasp anything coherent.

"Welcome back, Megan."

Craning her neck, she looked across the small room.

A wooden kitchen chair sat in the middle of the room, another brown item bobbing around in a sea of beige.

She remembered. She wasn't dreaming, she was in a waking nightmare.

Megan tried to move but couldn't. Pain lit up her body like Christmas lights, burning in her side, thumping in her head, weighing down her aching bones. She realised with growing apprehension that her arms were bent behind her head, her wrists lashed to the iron frame of the small bed.

She was back in the guest room, and she was a prisoner once more.

Her heart hammered in her chest, and she willed herself to calm down. She needed to think straight. She could figure this out.

Fingers clicked nearby.

Turning her head again, she locked eyes with the figure in the chair.

Ma sat watching her.

The woman's face was stony, but the slump of her shoulders was even more pronounced than it had been previously. There was a sadness in her eyes, too, that couldn't be hidden.

"Glad I have your attention," Ma said.

She held out an arm and opened her hand. The silver chain dropped and swung from her gnarled fingers.

A couple of the letters were now straight thanks to Megan's manipulation of the metal to aid in her escape. But there was no denying that it was the same piece of jewellery.

"Where did you get this?" asked Ma.

Megan blinked, confused.

"I found it," she croaked, the words thick in her throat, her voice like sandpaper. "I found it hidden behind the wallpaper, so I used it to escape." Memories from the basement crept into her mind, and she choked back a sob as the image flashed in her head of the girl collapsing to the ground without her face. "I should have just left and got help. Maybe then Lauren would still be alive. Oh God! I fucked up."

"Lauren?" Ma asked sharply.

Megan raised her eyes to Ma again as more memories flashed through her mind like still shots from a movie.

"You called her Tilly. Was she your daughter? Jesus fucking Christ! What the fuck was your daughter doing locked up in the basement?? You told me she'd died!"

"I thought she was dead!" Ma barked at her.

Megan shrank back against the mattress, frightened by the vehemence in the old woman's voice.

Ma glared at her for a moment. Her shoulders sagged, and all of a sudden, her body folded as she collapsed in on herself, like a balloon deflating.

"They told me she was dead. They needed more sons. The Brogan boys are what keeps the clan going. They took her from me when she was old enough. But the bloodline is too close and none of the children survived. They told me she had died in childbirth. If I had known she was still down there, I . . ."

"You would have done nothing," spat Megan. "You let those animals take your daughter – their daughter, their sister – to the basement to . . . to fucking procreate?! You should have saved her then. You're no better than they are. Do you eat people too? Do you know they're butchering that poor man's body down there? All he tried to do was save me."

Her fear had been replaced with anger, a white-hot rage that burned for that poor, innocent girl. For Liam O'Keefe. For herself.

Megan watched Ma's shoulders shake as she sobbed into her hands.

"And you're going to let them do it all over again. To me," she added quietly.

Ma lifted her head and scrubbed the tears from her face.

"Let them? How do you think I ended up here in the first place, Megan? Don't be so fucking naïve." She tossed the silver chain across the room.

Megan flinched as it bounced against her skin and slid to the floor with a metallic tinkle. The cogs turned in her brain as she looked from the chain to Ma, and back again.

And then the penny finally dropped.

32. Lauren Sees

The basement was every bit as horrifying as she had expected it to be. A damp, stinking mattress on the floor was all she had to sleep on, a couple of rough and tattered blankets all she had for comfort.

There was a bed down here, though.

She had seen it.

In the room at the end of the hall stood a single iron bed.

Lashed to the bed most of the time was another woman.

Crying in the corner of the room was that woman's son.

She had learned quickly to play nice with the men who came down regularly and soon noticed that the worst of their attention strayed towards the foreign girl in the iron bed. As she lay cowering on her filthy mattress, listening to the thumps, the screams, the squeaking iron bed in the next room, she tried to hold on to the image of her old self, that girl filled with hope who had hidden her name, hidden herself behind the wallpaper upstairs.

The longer she was here, the more that girl faded away.

When she had hidden the chain a few months back, she swore she was shedding her identity. She had been lying to herself then, but not anymore.

In this subterranean pit of horror, she knew that Lauren really had died. All that remained for now was this nameless shell that once housed a person with hopes and dreams.

As time wore on, the screams from the other room bothered her less and less.

She shouted through the metal door to the girl when the men weren't around, tried to strike up conversation, but the other woman was hysterical most of the time. And she didn't speak great English.

Still, though, she tried.

She knew that at any moment, their attention could turn back to her. Those fleeting moments of realisation reminded her that the real her was still in there, deep inside her. Terrified of what was still to come.

She supposed it was that part of her, the human part that still remained, that sought a connection with the other captive. If they were to face the horror here, let them not have to face it alone.

The other girl was Italian, that much had been divulged. On a holiday in Ireland with her five-year-old son, Vincenzo, when her car had broken down in the mountains. The men who had rescued them both were the monsters that held them now.

Thankfully, the men spoke kindly to the boy. She listened through the thin walls as slowly, his weeping ceased. His mother was usually too hysterical to notice him, and soon he stopped noticing her in return.

One of the men had become quite enamoured with Lauren. He would forego his time with the Italian woman to sit alongside her on the dirty mattress and talk.

She still feared him, and occasionally he gave her reason to, but she felt like they were beginning to understand one another. If she could build on that relationship, maybe things could be better here. She was never getting out, that much was clear to her, but could she thrive in an environment like this?

Not too long ago, the thought would have been inconceivable, but now, it seemed this place was hardening her heart and turning her into a monster too.

On the days when his eyes were kind and his voice gentle, she would tell him how uncomfortable she was. So, he brought her a bed with a clean mattress and fresh blankets.

She mentioned casually how horrid it was to wash herself in a bucket of cold water. He then brought her upstairs to shower, and although he showered with her and forced her to repay his act of kindness with acts of her own, the feeling of hot, soapy water on her body was blissful.

She had managed to successfully shut off the part of her brain that told her she was a victim. It was easier to stomach what she was becoming. She told herself that she wasn't suffering.

She was surviving.

The man's eyes weren't always kind, though, nor was his voice always gentle. Sometimes, more often than not, he watched her with icy eyes and spoke with his fists, his feet . . . anything he could use to demean her. To destroy her.

And then, on one of his good evenings, she'd told him wistfully about how lonely she was down here. He had stood quietly and left the room, and she mentally berated herself for pissing him off. His sudden, silent retreat left her with a sense of foreboding. Every part of her knotted in tension as the door across the hall unlocked.

All hell broke loose in the other room.

She cringed beneath the tattered blankets as the Italian woman screamed like a banshee, her anguished cries seeping into the walls and through them, haunting the basement.

"Non il mio bambino!" *screamed the woman.* "Non prendere mio figlio!"

The boy cried out. Bangs and scuffling sounds were drowned out as the woman's wailing increased in frequency. Overhead, the dogs began to bark and howl.

Still, she screamed.

"Vincenzo! Vin . . . VIN!"

A loud crack stilled the Italian woman's screams and the silence that followed was so heavy, she could feel it pressing down on her from where she cowered in her own room.

Footsteps approached.

The door opened and the man reappeared.

Perched on his hip, his head buried against the man's shoulder, was the boy.

As he tried to lower the child to the mattress, the boy clung to him. She watched quietly, the blankets now pooled on the floor around her.

"Hey, it's okay. I promise this lady is very nice. I'll go get some new toys. I bet she'll play with you."

The boy lifted his head and gazed at the man before turning his huge, dark eyes towards her. He was a beautiful child, all olive skin and dark hair, and despite herself, she felt a rush of emotion as she held his gaze.

She held out her arms and the boy threw himself into them, squeezing her tightly. Wiping a stray tear from her cheek with a free hand, she silently promised the boy, his mother, the entire universe that she would protect him like he was her own. That she would show him the affection he was so clearly missing.

"It's okay, Vin," she said, smoothing the dark locks of hair from his tear-stained face. "Everything will be fine. You can call me—"

"Ma. You can call her Ma," said the man as he turned to leave. He paused in the doorway and glanced back at her. The boy had stopped trembling but still held her tightly. The man smiled affectionately at the child before speaking once more, "And you can call him Finn. He's a Brogan now."

33. Animals Masquerading as Men

"I was only sixteen when they took me."

Megan watched quietly as Ma spoke, afraid to move lest the spell be broken.

"I know I look old, but it's this place that has aged me. Sucked the life right from me. I think I was forty on my last birthday, but that hardly matters anymore. My parents sent me over to Wicklow from the UK, to a camp for wayward teens. I wasn't a bad kid, mind you. Maybe a little wild. But even a little wild is too much for parents with high expectations. I hated the camp. The counsellors treated us like we were wild animals, and some of the other kids behaved as though they were. There was one counsellor in particular who terrified me. I don't recall his name, but I'll never forget his face or how he smelled as he crawled into my bunk each night. So, I ran away. Anywhere would be safer than that place. At least, that's what I thought."

Ma's eyes drifted closed, her face etched in a pain that was still fresh in her mind.

"If you think this place is rural now, you should have seen it back then. I got completely turned around on those country roads. And then I met Shay.

"He took me here, fed me, sheltered me. People from the camp came knocking on doors locally, looking for me. Shay lied for me. Protected me from them. I was so grateful. Until he expected me to show my gratitude much the same way as that disgusting man at camp.

"There was another girl here at the time. I didn't even know she existed until they brought me to the basement. She was Italian. A tourist who had been 'rescued' by Shay and Dominic. Not unlike you. That Italian girl, Georgia was her name, had a child, a little boy. Broke my heart to watch what they put her through. None of it was nice, but it was worse for her because she couldn't protect her son. She disappeared inside herself and left that child to fend for himself, but Shay and the others, they took a shine to him. Boys are special around here. They're revered. Still, no child should have to see the things he did. It changed him. Eventually, the Italian girl died, and it was my turn to fulfil their needs. There comes a point, Megan, where you have to decide if you want to exist or if you want to live. I wanted to live. I accepted my situation, and things got a whole lot better for me. They aren't perfect by any means, but they are better than what I was facing. When I had Tilly, I never suspected that they'd take her away when she came of age. She was their blood as much as she was mine. I had another girl afterwards, and I did what I had to do to protect her. I couldn't protect Matilda, but I saw to it that they'd never take another daughter from my arms to harm. It was better for her. This place offers no life to girls. Only pain and death.

"I wish I had the chance to tell Michael the truth before you murdered him. He loved me as a boy loves their grandmother, but he always felt the loss of a mother he didn't know, one who abandoned him. I don't know how he would have felt if he had known I was his mother. Denny always was a nasty one. Nastier even than Dominic, and Lord, how I wish that man would die roaring."

She looked at Megan, her face impassive but her eyes burning with pain and anger. Megan couldn't begin to imagine what she had suffered at the hands of these animals masquerading as men.

"I'm so sorry, Lauren. I never meant to hurt Michael. I just wanted to live. I wanted to rescue the girl in the basement. I wish I had been able to save her. I wish I could save you," she whispered, tears tracking along her face. "You need to help me get out of here. I know you feel guilt and regret for Tilly. You can make amends. You can help me get out of this place!"

"The only way I can help you, Megan, is to give you some advice: the sooner you submit and accept that your life has changed, the easier this will be. I'm almost envious. At least you have Finn. He's handsome, smart, and he'll make sure the others stay away from you. You could have a good life here. And you'd have me. I didn't have the luxury of a female companion."

"Luxury?? There is no luxury to be had here," Megan said, her voice rising as anger and desperation consumed her. "You're nothing more than a slave! I refuse to be someone's possession! What would you do if you had the chance to save Tilly? To get her away from this place? Would you take it? Because you are the only chance I have at surviving, Lauren. Do you think Tilly would be proud of her mother for standing by and watching another girl waste away here? Unloved and forgotten?"

Ma bolted from the chair, the wooden frame tipping over in her haste. She pointed a shaking finger at Megan, her eyes burning with fury.

"She WAS loved! She will NEVER be forgotten!" she hissed.

"Then help me. For Tilly," Megan pleaded.

Ma reached behind her and righted the upturned chair. Without warning, she dropped heavily onto it, her body shaking as she started to sob. Megan watched her quietly, silently imploring the broken woman before her to do the right thing. She was Megan's only hope. Eventually, her sobs subsided, and Ma brushed her hair back from her face. Her eyes rose to meet Megan's.

"Okay," she said.

Megan looked at her with disbelief. Hope slowly crept back into her body, dulling the varying sensations of pain. "You'll help me?" she asked hopefully.

Ma sighed heavily and nodded her head.

"Yes. I'll help you. For Tilly. For Georgia, the Italian girl. For all the women these bastards have hurt across the generations. I'll help you. But you need to do exactly as I say."

Nodding enthusiastically, Megan wanted nothing more than to jump from the bed and hug the daylights out of the woman in front of her. Ma. Lauren. It didn't matter. She was going to help her escape.

With a quick glance towards the door, Ma continued. "They will come for you soon. They'll take you to the basement. I need you to fight just a little. Just enough that they won't suspect anything. I will arrive shortly behind you. I'll have a weapon. Don't be alarmed by anything I say. The moment their guard is down, I'll take care of them.

I don't give a shit about Shay or Denny. In fact, if I get the chance, I will happily kill them both. But not Ollie. I won't hurt my son. Or Finn. But I will incapacitate them long enough for you to escape."

Megan nodded again, her eyes wide as she tried to make sense of the strange family dynamic. If Lauren wasn't Finn's mother, then who was?

She didn't dare ask, fearing she already knew the answer.

It certainly explained why he stood out among the Brogans.

A rose among weeds. Beautiful, but prepared to cause pain to any unsuspecting person who got close enough to feel those hidden thorns tear at their flesh.

34. Lauren Loses

"*Do you need anything, Ma?*"

Finn leaned down and rested a tender hand against her cheek. He subtly wiped her tears away, and she silently thanked him for it.

"*No, Finn. We're okay. We just need some rest, is all. You're a good boy, though. You've always been a good boy.*"

The handsome young man before her grinned and patted her hand. "You've always been a good ma too. Get some rest. I'll be back in a bit to check in on you. And this little angel." He stroked the baby's cheek and gazed lovingly down at his infant sister. After a moment, he turned on his heels and left the room, closing the door gently behind him.

She fell back heavily against the pile of pillows and sighed. It felt as though it reverberated right through her very soul. Against her chest, the baby grumbled, her tiny fists waving angrily like a little old man shouting at clouds. Ma readjusted in the bed and slipped the nightdress off her shoulder. Gently, she guided the infant to her exposed breast. The tiny girl latched on greedily and Ma dropped back heavily again.

Her body still ached.

Childbirth was a miracle, but it was still something she dreaded. It was hard on a woman, even harder still out here in the mountains with no real medical assistance. No pain relief. No qualified doctor to ease her fears if something felt wrong. Just a sea of male faces telling her to push. She had already lost a few babies over the years. It was probably a blessing in disguise, though. She knew how they would be raised here.

She thought of Michael.

His birth was the most recent successful one, although he didn't know she was his mother. As far as that boy was concerned, his father had told him that his mother abandoned them both. Wasn't he lucky to have such a great grandma, though?

She played her role. She wished to tell him the truth, and had come close so many times, but the warning in Denny's dead eyes was always blatant and plain to see.

So, she played at being Grandma and cherished every cuddle, every story, every second she got to spend with her beautiful boy. His conception had brought her great suffering, and the shame still burned hotly on her cheeks if she recalled it, but the moment she laid eyes on his wizened pink face as he burst screaming into this world, all the pain melted away.

As it had with Matilda.

A sob wrenched from her chest at the thought of her beautiful daughter. At her breast, the baby lost its rhythm and began to grizzle. She readjusted and the suckling commenced. The child was content once more.

Matilda had been a beautiful child. Ma wasn't quite sure which of the men had fathered her. She hoped it was Shay because of them all, he was the kindest to her. Despite his darkness, he had some light in him. He had given Finn to her all those years ago. Perhaps it was her proximity to

Finn coupled with his adoration of the boy, but ever since that day, Shay had treated her like a human.

Unlike the rest of his family.

As Tilly had grown, Ma watched perplexed as he grew colder towards the child. Still, she never suspected a thing until the girl became a teenager. She woke one night to the sounds of screams. Denny had decided the time was right and the girl was of age. It was time for her to fulfil her purpose within the Brogan household.

Ma had screamed and shouted at him. Tilly was not much more than a child. She was a part of this family. She was his . . . what? His sister? His daughter? She honestly didn't know, but he didn't seem to care in any regard.

Women were animals to Denny. Meat. Something to be chewed up and spat out.

Shay had tried to calm her, but there was no calming the storm that raged within her. That had been the worst night in a long, long time. She came to days later with broken ribs, a fractured wrist, and more cuts and bruises than she cared to try to count. Shay explained to her calmly but firmly that it was time for Matilda to do her part for the family. The Brogan line needed more sons if it was to carry on. Her heart shattered. Each time he informed her that Tilly was with child, her heart shattered. Each time he told her that another child had been lost, her heart shattered. She knew why the children weren't surviving, but nobody listened when she said so. They were confident that their seed was strong enough to overcome all. Eventually, she stopped asking about Tilly, until the day Shay told her that a particularly difficult birth had killed not just the infant, but Matilda too. Ma was afraid to ask about her beautiful girl, about how the end had been. Too afraid that every time she thought of her daughter, she would see her dark ending instead of the light she had brought to Ma every day of her short life.

That was the day she really died inside.

She always thought it had happened long before but could never pinpoint the exact moment she just never quite felt like she was alive in this place.

It turned out she was very much alive. But the death of her only daughter at the hands of a monster – these monsters – well, that was the thing that finally snuffed out whatever light was left burning within her.

And now she faced the same thing all over again.

As she gazed down at the perfect little girl in her arms, the child's life as a Brogan flashed through her mind like a movie reel. Ma knew exactly where things were headed.

As life had stirred within her with the conception of the as-yet-unnamed baby girl, so too had life begun to stir in the hollow husk of her heart. With every hiccup and kick from the baby, her own heart had flourished and grown whole again. It would continue to do so over the years until they took it all away again and killed her.

The only thing more difficult than dying was doing it over and over again.

Ma knew what she needed to do, and with tears in her eyes she kissed the little girl's fuzzy head and inhaled her soft scent.

Then she pulled the infant close to her chest, covering her little face completely.

The child, too tiny to struggle, too innocent to understand, stayed put.

Ma's arms trembled with the strain. This was surely the heaviest burden she had ever carried.

Her streaming tears became wracking sobs, and finally, she lifted the infant away from her breast. The baby lay limply in her mother's arms.

She looked eerily like a perfectly formed doll with her delicate, porcelain skin, her rosebud lips, her unmoving chest.

As her heart cracked and shrivelled within her once more, Ma consoled herself that she had done the right thing. Better for the baby to suffer for a brief moment now, than to suffer immeasurably in the future. And at the hands of those she would grow to love.

The door swung inward, and Finn burst into the room, concern etched on his face.

"What's happened, Ma? Calm down." He raced to her side, his face freezing as realisation dawned, but still he reached out and gently took the dead child from her arms and placed it in the crib before enveloping Ma in his embrace.

Finn shouted towards the open door to alert the others, and it was only then, as his words failed to penetrate the shrill sound that flooded her ears, that Ma realised her own mouth was moving too.

From someplace deep inside her tortured mind, she wondered idly how long she had been screaming.

35. Are You Ready?

"I just wish you could see how much I care about you. I only have your best interests at heart."

Megan rolled her eyes and stared at Finn, seething.

When she heard footsteps approaching after Ma had left her, Megan prepared herself for what would follow.

The Brogan men would come. They would take her to the basement. She would fight, but only enough to avoid suspicion. Her body thrummed with anticipation and anxiety. She had no idea what Ma had planned to aid her escape, but all she could do was place her trust in the woman. She knew this place well. Knew these monsters well. Megan still couldn't believe that the mysterious Lauren had been hiding in plain sight all this time.

It wasn't the men.

At least not all of them.

The footsteps had preceded Finn.

He dipped his head into the room cautiously. Why he was behaving in such a careful manner, she didn't understand. She was strapped to the goddamned bed, so it wasn't like she could attack him.

But as he had begun to try to worm his way back into her good graces, she understood his caution. He really thought he could shift her perspective. While she lay tied to a bed with a lump on her head from the whack he had given her with a baseball bat.

Hush, my darling.

Her stomach twisted as she listened to him state his case. How had she not seen how crazy he was? She saw something in his eyes, a darkness maybe, but not the full-blown crazy he was showing her now. He was laying all his cards on the table, so to speak, as he spoke wistfully of the future they would have together. Children, more dogs, maybe even a small cabin out back that would be just for them. Nobody would touch her because she would be his wife for all intents and purposes.

"'My best interests'? Allowing your family to assault me would be in my best interests? Maybe a little rape here and there too? Will we have the occasional family barbecue, Finn? Maybe feast on the flesh of those who have crossed us? You make me sick. Your whole fucking twisted family makes me sick!" she yelled.

From his place on the floor by the bed, Ted whined.

Megan hated that she was stressing the dog. He was the only good thing about this place.

"No, Megan." Finn sighed, clearly exasperated by her unwillingness to see his point of view. "They won't touch you. Ask Ma. Nobody laid a hand on her after Da claimed her. You'll be safe with me. I promise you. As for the meat, I understand it's a difficult pill to swallow, but I told you before: we live off the land here as much as we can. This place was founded by Brogan men way back when. The land was cursed with a great hunger, and people ate whatever they could find. Sustenance is sustenance. We don't believe in waste. And we do believe in tradition." He reached out and touched her face tenderly, his eyes soft.

She knew Finn was lying. Knew Ma had suffered at the hands of Dominic and Denny long after Shay had "claimed her". But to tell him so could jeopardise her new alliance. What would they do to Ma if they knew she had spoken so candidly with their newest captive? Frustration and anger bubbled beneath her skin like a disease.

Without warning, Megan retched up a wad of phlegm and spat in his face.

Finn reeled back and slapped her hard.

The dog jumped to its feet and started to bark, throwing its barrel-shaped body between its master and the girl in the bed. The poor canine's loyalties were being pushed to the limit. Megan knew that despite the monster she now knew him to be, Finn loved that dog wholeheartedly. He wouldn't want to see the creature in distress.

Sure enough, Finn straightened, hissing air through his teeth in frustration. He knelt down and pulled Ted close to him, petting the dog until it calmed.

"Have it your way. It won't take too long before you see that I was right. I'm the safest place for you here, Megan."

He turned on his heel and stalked out, tapping his leg for the dog to follow.

Ted whined once more and licked Megan's face before trotting out of the room after his master.

The door closed, but the lock didn't click, and Megan understood that her time was almost up. They were coming for her. This was the crux of her predicament, and she could only hope that it would play out in her favour.

They came in a flurry of heavy boot steps and quiet murmurs. Shay and Denny moved towards her cautiously as though approaching a cornered animal. Ollie stood by the door, his eyes dancing with excitement, ready to clear the way for the others as they transported their precious cargo to a more secure destination.

Megan felt sick.

Nervous energy vibrated through her entire body. She tried so hard to hold on to her logic, to maintain enough presence of mind to behave accordingly. Panic was setting in, and she fought it with everything she could. Whatever happened, however rough they were with her, however much they goaded her, there was one thing she would not do.

She would not scream.

She would not give them the satisfaction. She wouldn't give them the excitement. A scream would be like ringing the dinner bell. Like a drop of blood falling through the ocean, attracting the sharks. Like throwing a steak to a starving dog.

She would not scream.

Shay held her limbs tightly as Denny untied the bindings. She pitched her body, thrashing and twisting away from them, but she was careful not to do it *too much*. She didn't want to risk pissing anyone off. She couldn't afford any kind of physical retribution for her actions. A clear head and minimal injuries would be critical to her escape.

Tears rolled down her cheek, and she held Ollie's gaze, avoiding looking at either of the men closest to her. Ollie didn't seem as dangerous as the others. He was still a sick freak as far as Megan was concerned, but there was a foolish innocence about him all the same.

As they manhandled her through the door and along the hallway, she struggled. It was enough to make them lift her off the floor and carry her among them, Ollie still leading the way to open doors as needed. Foolish innocence.

As they dragged her through the basement door and down the steps, Denny manoeuvred her the wrong way, bashing her head off the bare brick wall.

She winced. But still, she didn't cry out.

The disappointment on his face was evident, and it gave her a small kernel of satisfaction. It warmed her. It fuelled her for what was to come.

The route was familiar to her, and she knew exactly where they were taking her. As they rounded the corner, the room where Tilly had been held came into view. The door was open, and Finn stood by it, his mouth set in a grim line.

As they hauled her past him, Megan wondered idly if he was bothered more by his family manhandling her or by her unwillingness to accept his twisted form of chivalry.

It hardly mattered now anyway.

She was tossed upon a new bed, sliding along the surface as her body hit the mattress. Her fingers touched plastic. Instead of regular linen, there was rubber sheeting on the bed. The implication twisted her stomach into knots, and she felt her gorge rise.

Ted padded into the room, heading straight to her bedside where he dropped heavily to the floor and settled down to sleep. She still felt warmed by the dog's presence.

Silent tears continued to fall from her closed eyes as they strapped her down. Her heart hammered in her chest as she considered the new bindings. They were leather straps, just like the kind of thing she had seen in every horror movie ever based in psychiatric hospitals. As the buckles were bound and tightened, Megan shuddered. Her whole body trembled. Fear. Nerves. Anticipation. She didn't know which, but she knew that Ma was nowhere to be seen. That kernel of hope inside her was beginning to wither and die.

And then a sound.

A metallic grinding drew nearer.

Someone – she didn't know who, so entrenched in her fear was she – adjusted something behind her in the bed that lifted her head and shoulders just enough to provide a view of the dingy hallway outside.

Ma approached, a long-handled axe hanging at her side. Tiny sparks leapt from the cement floor as she approached. Megan stared, transfixed by the scene as it unfolded.

She felt better now that Ma was here. The end was so close. It was a tangible thing. Megan licked her cracked lips as she pondered how messy things would get with an axe involved. How would Ma incapacitate her boys with an axe without killing them?

The woman came to a stop at the foot of the bed and regarded Megan without expression. Should she offer her a smile? No, that would surely alert the men.

Was she supposed to wait for some kind of sign?

"Are you ready?" Shay said to nobody in particular.

All the air seemed to have been sucked from the room, and Megan's eyes darted from one person to the next.

Ma hefted the axe and stepped forward.

"I'm sorry, Megan," she said, though her eyes said she was anything but. "I'm a part of this family. I'm a Brogan now. And so are you."

The axe whistled through the air and hit Megan's leg with a sickening crack.

This time, she did scream.

36. After All This Time

"No, Killian! What has Mommy told you about those? They are very, very dangerous, my love."

Megan hobbled through the long grass and gently redirected her son's hand. "These are called death cap mushrooms. See the way they almost have a greenish tint to them? And they feel slimy. Yuck! You must never touch."

The boy giggled, and Megan's heart tightened.

"Let's pick some garlic now. We have enough mushrooms."

Killian raced across the clearing and threw himself among the patches of garlic. The tiny white flowers danced lazily as a soft breeze blew through the forest.

It was so peaceful here.

If she tried really hard, she could almost forget everything for a few moments, forget the last six years and pretend as though she were back home. Just a normal family outing in the forest, like the ones she had taken so many times with her dad.

She sighed and grasped her cane tighter as she limped across to join her little boy as he plucked the verdant green stalks from the ground carefully like she had shown him so many times.

The sun tracked its way westward slowly as mother and son made their way back through the trees. Killian held her hand tightly, conscious of moving slowly so his mommy could keep up. Even at five years old he understood that movement was more difficult for someone with only one leg.

The healing process from the amputation had been difficult. It left deep scars on her body and even deeper ones on her soul. She didn't think she'd ever forget the sickly smell of burning flesh from the cauterisation. Even worse was the burning smell that followed when they'd carved up her lower leg and feasted on the roasted flesh.

More difficult than all of that, was the process of relearning how to adjust to life without her leg. She knew they had taken it for control. The same reason they had taken everything else.

"Careful in the mud, baby," she said softly as they breached the tree line around the Brogan homeplace. Despite the brightness of the day, a shadow fell across her as soon as she stepped back across the property line. The forest provided her with a sense of freedom. A false sense, but one she felt, nonetheless. Being back in this place minimised her. All the good things shrivelled away and receded into the darkest corners of her mind. It was like the land was cursed. Nothing good could grow here. At that last thought, she glanced at her son and her heart constricted.

What kind of life would he have here?

As a boy, he would be safe. But what of the people he would meet throughout his life? What kind of person would he become, living among these people? What kind of pain would he inflict? Wiping a stray tear from her cheek, Megan huffed to a stop beside him, lowering the basket of foraged flora to the rutted earth.

Killian had stopped, as he always did, by the rose bush next to the barn. He reached out, as he always did, and fingered the silver chain that hung, hidden within the folds of its spindly branches. The chain was weatherworn and tarnished now, but seeing it always brought a wry smile to Megan's face.

Ma, or Lauren, as Megan had insisted on calling her once she was allowed to rejoin the household, had never grown any warmer towards her. She had been cold in life, and Megan assumed she was just as cold now in death.

There was no bonding over shared experience, no words of comfort. Knowing what she knew, Megan wasn't surprised. She didn't take it personally. The woman had been through so much. Her empathy had died long ago. When empathy is gone, all we have left to lose is our humanity. And nothing good would grow there.

A piercing wail broke the stillness, and Megan's heart began to race.

"Time to go, buster," she said, grasping her son's pudgy hand in her own and moving towards the house as quickly as she could with just one leg and an old wooden stick.

As they rounded the corner, the crying stopped suddenly. With a galloping heart, Megan stumbled towards the porch steps just as the front door opened.

Finn stepped out, his infant daughter held in the crook of his arm.

His face lit up as he watched their approach, and he knelt down slowly, careful not to jostle his little girl. Killian screeched in delight and ran to his father. The small boy, a carbon copy of Finn with his dark hair and soul-penetrating, stormy grey eyes, started to talk a mile a minute, telling his father about how helpful he was on their foraging trip. Finn smiled affectionately at his son and ruffled his mop of dark hair before meeting Megan's eyes over the top of their son's head. He smiled warmly at her.

Megan smiled back.

She moved forward, reaching out for her daughter. Finn plucked the basket stuffed with mushrooms, garlic, and a multitude of herbs from her with one arm as he passed the baby across with the other.

"Daisy has been the best girl," he said with a smile as he hoisted Killian into his arms. "She woke up a couple of minutes ago, though. She was pretty angry, so I didn't want to leave her. She just needed a cuddle."

Leaning down to kiss her daughter's head, Megan inhaled that heady baby scent that made her insides flutter every single time. "What time do we need to leave for her appointment?" she asked casually.

The atmosphere changed instantly, and as she turned to look at Finn, Megan's heart dropped to her stomach.

Something was wrong.

"About that," he said evenly. "Ollie is really sick. Worse than he was this morning. I think we're going to have to postpone."

Megan rounded on him.

"You can't be serious, Finn? You promised me that we could get her shots done. You know it would make me feel better. I'm sorry Ollie is unwell, but let's face it, he was only coming as an extra set of eyes for me. To guard me. Have I not given everything to you these past few years? And still, you won't even take me off this mountain just this one time. Like you promised."

Megan knew she was edging close to the line.

Pissing him off was the last thing she wanted to do, but she had been preparing for this for too long. She had been through too much in this place. With this family.

She'd be damned if she was going to let her children go through it too. Especially Daisy.

It might have worked for Lauren, but death as a release wasn't an option for Megan. There was no freedom in death.

Glancing at her son and daughter, she tried to quell the panic that was rising within her. It had been a massive risk to use the death cap mushrooms on Ollie, but she wasn't stupid.

They had worked on Lauren; they would work on him.

She knew this could be her only opportunity to get herself and her children out. She had too much to live for. She couldn't fuck this up now. She wouldn't bury her head in the sand like Lauren had for all those years. Sure, she would have liked more time to prepare, to build their trust in her, but she had Daisy to think of.

And the new girl in the basement.

Reaching out with her free arm, Megan grabbed the front of Finn's shirt and pulled him towards her. Pressing her forehead against his chest, she sighed heavily.

"I'm sorry, but I haven't seen anything beyond this place in so long, Finn. How am I ever supposed to be happy here if you won't trust me? I'm supposed to be your wife, not your prisoner."

He stood motionless for a moment before exhaling heavily and kissing the top of her head. "You're right, Meg. That's not fair to you at all. You've given up a lot, and I appreciate it." He squeezed her arm. "Fine. We'll go into town. A promise is a promise. I love you, Meg."

"I love you too."

It took everything, just as it always did, not to spit the words at him. But keeping up appearances was the only thing that had gotten her to this point. She had stepped outside herself for the past six years. Finn believed that they were a happy little family.

Hell, at times, she almost allowed herself to believe it too. She was certain that he had no idea of the resentment she harboured. She hated him with every fibre of her being. Hated the whole family.

There had been some good through the years, though.

Ted had soon come to see Megan as his master.

The Labrador had been as consistent as her shadow, always by her side. The constant presence, the unadulterated love that the old dog had for her, those were the things that got her through those first blisteringly lonely weeks and months. As she navigated her new position, her new body, Ted had been there every slow and shuffling step of the way.

All too soon, though, Ted was the one shuffling. They would stroll around the backyard, Megan eventually noticing that the dog was struggling to keep up despite her physical disadvantage.

Suddenly, he was struggling with the few steps that led from the porch to the front door. The scars still crisscrossed her only knee from the time she had tried to help the dog up the steps. He wasn't a slim dog by any means, and his weight had caused them both to stagger.

Megan, still growing used to her lack of mobility, had fallen hard on the gravel yard, the weight of the dog grinding her skin onto the ground.

The reduced movement was soon followed by low, keening howls. Megan had watched in fear as he had begun to walk into cupboards and walls that had been there all his life, as though they no longer existed. Finn had sat her down and explained that the most likely culprit was a massive tumour on the dog's brain. The keening, he explained, was due to the huge pressure that was slowly building in the dog's cranium. The kindest thing to do was to put Ted out of his misery.

As she watched the Brogan family rally around the sick dog, the irony wasn't lost on her.

These people would treat their fellow humans like animals. There was never an option for their victims to be put out of their misery.

And so, that same night, as the weather raged outside, mirroring the tumult of emotions that Megan was feeling, she sat on the kitchen floor with Ted.

The dog lay cradled in her arms as Finn began administering the cocktail of drugs that would lead the dog to first fall peacefully asleep, before finally delivering a fatal dose of chemicals to stop his heart.

The heart that had been given so fully and so freely to Megan with no expectation or reciprocity required.

She had stroked Ted's head as he gazed soulfully into her eyes. Tears wet her cheeks and she had wept into his soft, brown coat as his eyes slowly closed for the final time. She sobbed, her hands twisting into the fur around his neck when Finn had depressed the plunger on the syringe. Slow and heavy breaths had continued huffing from the sleeping dog, until finally he stilled completely.

Finn had patted Ted's head and stood, squeezing Megan's shoulder as he passed her. The kitchen door had closed gently behind him, and she found herself grateful to him for giving her these final moments to grieve alone.

"What's the matter, darling?"

Shaking herself from the reverie she had slipped into, Megan lifted her eyes to Finn. He reached out and wiped a tear from her cheek.

"Just thinking about Ted," she said, offering him a watery smile.

He leaned forward again and kissed her tenderly on the cheek.

"He was the goodest of good doggos," he whispered.

"Did somebody say doggo?"

The front door clattered closed behind Denny, startling Daisy who began to wail again.

Rolling her eyes, Megan rocked the little girl gently until her cries subsided.

Tiny feet pattered along the floor and Daisy jolted again as Killian cried out with glee.

"A puppy! Is he for me, Uncle Denny?"

"He is, indeed, my boy," said Denny, eying his nephew with delight.

Killian threw himself to the floor and scooped up the chunky puppy. Its soft fur was mostly black, except for his tan socks and moustache. A thin stripe of white ran from the top of his head and along his snout, blooming into a snowy chest plate. A tiny pink stripe edged his snuffling nose, and despite herself, Megan's heart melted as she watched her son gently lift the small dog in the air and kiss its head.

"That's a Bernese mountain dog, Killian. He's only little now, but mark my words, he'll be a big boy when he's grown. Just like you! Now tell us, what are you gonna call your new pal?"

The young boy's tongue poked from his mouth as he considered the question with the brevity that only a five-year-old could afford such a simple query.

After a moment, Killian lifted his head and beamed at his uncle.

"Moose," he said. "I'm gonna call him Moose. You said he'll be big, and I read in a book once that they're really big. It's a good name."

Denny crowed with laughter, delighted with his nephew. "*Maith an buachill*! It's a great name! Welcome to the family, Moose!"

"Killian! Time to go, sweetie."

Rummaging through the baby bag, sure that she had everything she needed, Megan swung it onto her shoulder and hobbled out through the front door.

If everything went to plan, it would be the last time she ever had to do so.

The thought was liberating.

Coos and giggles travelled on the breeze from the open car door. Finn was stooped forward securing Daisy in her seat. With a tug on the straps, he stood back and pulled faces at the baby, eliciting hearty chuckles as she waved her pudgy fists in delight.

She watched quietly from the porch steps. For the millionth time, Megan wondered if she was making the right decision. He loved the children so dearly, and they him. And he had been good to her. Mostly.

Yet, she was still a prisoner. And although she couldn't imagine Finn allowing the rest of his family to lock his daughter up to be used like an animal in the future, she wasn't willing to hang around and take that risk.

Not after Matilda.

A small shape darted across the yard and careened into Megan's leg, almost knocking her off balance. Bending down to scratch Moose behind the ears, she shielded her eyes from the afternoon sun and watched Killian as he raced after his new furry friend, kicking up a cloud of dust in his wake.

"C'mon, baby, we need to get going. Daisy has an appointment with the nurse," she said softly.

"Awww, Ma," the young boy groaned. "I want to play with Moose. Uncle Denny said this is the bonding time. What does bonding mean?"

Straightening, she chuckled and ruffled his hair.

"It means becoming friends. I'm sure Daddy would be okay with you bringing Moose along?" She glanced across at Finn, not liking the shadow that passed across his face.

"You can stay here with me, buachill. Town is boring. Especially the doctor's office."

Megan startled at Denny's voice over her shoulder, and her heart plummeted at his words.

"Hooray! Can I, Ma?" Killian beamed up at her, and Megan's heart shattered into a million fragments.

Both Denny and Finn watched her, and she fought to keep her face as neutral as possible, but she was fighting a losing battle. This was it. Her only chance to get out of here. To save herself. To save her children. To save the girl tied up in the basement.

Complacency had crept up on her over the past few years. Pretending that this was a normal life, a life she chose, made it easier to swallow. Until Dominic had pulled into the yard late one evening just a couple of weeks ago.

The stack lights on the top of the garda car had strobed blue, casting an eerie glow across the dreary walls inside the kitchen. The sirens had remained silent, though.

It was the first time Megan had ever seen the patrol lights on, and for a brief moment, her heart had lifted. Was she finally being rescued?

Until the men had all rushed to meet Dominic and helped to bundle the flailing girl inside and down to the basement as quickly as possible.

As they had filed through the hall, the girl had zeroed in on Megan, begging her to help.

Frozen in place by the kitchen door, Megan stared in shock into the dark eyes of the frightened girl. She looked no more than sixteen or seventeen. A runaway, she later overheard Dominic tell his nephews.

Denny had lost his grip on her, and sensing the freedom to move she tried to dart towards the door, but Dominic barred her way. The girl shrieked, and Megan watched, horrified, through someone else's eyes as her own mouth began to move and form words.

"The children are asleep, Finn," she hissed. "Please be quiet."

Finn had nodded and before she could blink, his fist connected with the girl's face. She slumped to the floor like a dead body. Silent.

The Brogan men had all turned to look at Megan, quiet approval in each of their faces, and something inside her, slick and wet, began to squirm. If she didn't get out of there, she would become no better than Lauren. No better than the Brogan men.

She could not allow her daughter to grow up in this household.

Killian would be safe here, though. The Brogans idolised him. He was one of their own. A prince among men.

But what would he become?

If she stayed, her daughter would be at risk for the rest of her life.

If she left, her son would become a monster.

But wouldn't he become one anyway?

A monster raised by monsters follows only one path in life. The only path they know to follow.

Swallowing a sob, Megan pulled her son close to her. She knew that if she left him here, she ran the risk of losing him forever. Breathing in deep, she let every part of him invade her senses. The smell of wild garlic that still clung to his dark hair. Those huge, chocolate-button eyes that she had drowned in so many times since she first held his tiny body in her arms. The dimples on his cheeks as his mouth stretched in a grin. "I love you so, so much, baby boy. Never forget it," she whispered against his ear.

Killian kissed her cheek and took off running with wild abandon, howling with glee as Moose the puppy lumbered after him.

"Why are you crying, Megan?"

She turned to Denny.

"It's the first time I'll have ever been away from Killian. Even if it is just for a short while. Please take care of him."

Denny's eyes searched her face, mistrust printed all over his own.

"I'll take care of him."

His words were comforting, but his eyes challenged her.

If the only tenderness Denny had ever shown was towards her son, that was good enough for her. She knew he would take care of Killian. Regardless of how he felt about her, or her about him, Megan knew that he adored his nephew.

With a shuddering breath, she turned and climbed awkwardly into the car.

37. Seeing in Colour

Anguish had followed her down off the mountain.

It had grown like a dreary cloud the further she travelled from her son. But still, Megan was awed as the land unfolded before them.

For six years, she had seen nothing but the Brogan house and the forest around it. It was as though the whole world beyond it had ceased to exist.

But now cars passed them by, growing in frequency the further away from the mountains they drove. A small village opened up and Megan pressed her nose against the glass as she watched the small town's occupants mill around, going about their daily lives like it was just your average Monday afternoon.

And to them, it was.

To Megan, it was potential freedom. An unlocked door offering escape from the nightmare she had lived in captivity for the past six years.

As the houses thinned out and the village fell away to more fields and more trees, she understood that Finn was taking her to one of the bigger towns by the coast. More people probably meant more risk for him, but it also offered the kind of anonymity that just didn't come with small towns.

Still, he seemed much more relaxed than she had expected. Especially considering Ollie's absence. It pleased her to think she had played her part well.

As they drove into town, Megan felt the first stirrings of anxiety. She hadn't figured on how overwhelming it would be to see so many people. The absence of something can never truly be felt until it returns and makes its presence known.

She watched through the glass as they crested a small hill, the sparkling blue sea suddenly stretching out before them. Below, the harbour framed the seascape, boats big and small bobbing on the water. Sails in every colour of the rainbow stood tall as the boats waited on the gently rocking water for their owners to take them out to sea. Swathes of green popped like bunches of flowers from between buildings as each small group of trees reached for the sun. A whitewashed steeple peeped through the trees in the near distance and through the open window on Finn's side of the car, church bells chimed and intermingled with the distant whoops and hollers of children at play. It was so beautiful, and Megan gasped in awe at the vibrancy of the town and its inhabitants. It felt like she was seeing in colour for the first time in a long time, and it fuelled her determination and hurt her heart in equal measure.

She turned her head towards Finn, embarrassed with herself for showing such overwhelm, but he just smiled and squeezed her knee with his free hand. Behind them, snug in her car seat, Daisy snored gently, unaware of her picturesque surroundings. Unaware of the turmoil her mother felt.

Finn turned into a small carpark at the bottom of the hill, right on the edge of the harbour.

Craning her neck to take in the area, Megan turned to him, confused. "Where's the doctor's office?"

"It's not too far. I thought the stroll would be nice. I know it's been a while since you've seen anything but the mountains," he said sheepishly. "I know it might be tough on you, physically like, but it's not often you get to do it."

Megan wished, and not for the first time, that they had met under other circumstances. That he was part of a different family. Deep down, she thought that maybe he was a decent man. In his own twisted way, he showed her so much love, and he worshipped their children. Deeper down still, though, he was a monster. She knew it. Had seen it with her own eyes. She glanced at the stump where her leg used to be.

But in moments like this, when he looked at her with that beautifully dark and intense gaze, she wished so hard for life to be normal. If his demons were exorcised, she could really love him.

And that made it all the more difficult to face up to what she needed to do.

The sun was warm on her skin as they walked along the harbour. Finn pushed the stroller, Daisy cooing at all the new sights. Megan hobbled alongside them, leaning on her cane more than usual. Daisy was a little grumpy when Megan lifted her sleeping form from the car seat, but the grizzling turned to beaming smiles almost immediately as the little girl eyed the boats, the screeching seagulls, the spark of life in her mother's eyes.

Conversation was minimal as they walked. Finn tried, but Megan's head was on a swivel as she took everything in with as much delight as her daughter. He laughed heartily when she spied the oversized cartoon ice cream cone outside a small shop.

She had squealed with delight. "Can we get ice cream before we go home?" she asked, realising quickly what she had said.

Home.

The thought made her shiver.

Finn's eyes had lit up, though, and he agreed that ice cream was a great idea. Her heart hurt knowing what was coming, but Megan tried to ignore it. No good would come from pulling at that thread.

Beside her, Finn stiffened, and she felt herself freeze as just ahead, two uniformed gardai stepped from a coffee shop, takeaway cups in hand, and crossed to their side of the road. His pace quickened, and Megan's mind started to spin. Was this her chance? Should she go for it now? Alert the two officers and beg for safety?

Still undecided, a cry for help frozen on her tongue, Megan watched as both officers – a young woman in her late twenties and a man not much older – slowed their pace. They eyed Megan and Finn, recognition clear on both of their faces. Hope bubbled inside her. This was it! They knew who she was. Someone was looking for her!

"Finn Brogan!" the female officer exclaimed, her face breaking into a warm smile. "I haven't seen you in an age!"

"What's the craic, Finno??" the other officer shouted, slapping Finn heartily on the shoulder.

Sneaking a surreptitious glance at Finn, Megan could see the clear panic in his eyes. She watched in astonishment as he masked it in a split second. He greeted both officers like old friends.

"Jason! Fiadh!"

Megan stood awkwardly as the trio chatted.

"And is this the wife, then?" asked Jason, eyeing Megan as though seeing her for the first time. She cringed as his gaze travelled lower to her missing limb.

"Aye. And this is our daughter. The young fella opted to stay home with Denny."

"Denny?" Jason crowed. "Jesus, I haven't seen that fucker in forever. Tell him I was asking for him, won't you? So where did you find this one?"

Finn froze, and Megan marvelled at the fact that he seemed so prepared for everything, and yet the simplest of questions appeared to have left him speechless. And then the two faces turned to her. Megan watched as inquisitiveness turned into something else on Fiadh's face, as though she had started to read the situation from pure vibes alone. Or maybe some kind of girl power telepathy.

And then a car was pulling alongside them, the horn blasting made them all jump. Daisy started to cry, and Megan rushed to comfort her daughter.

The awkward spell was broken.

The moment lost.

"The fuck are you doing standing around yacking?" barked Dominic from the patrol car.

The two officers straightened, but their heads hung low, suitably chastised.

"Just haven't seen Finn in a while, is all, sir," answered the officer called Jason. "Was just enquiring after him."

"Well enquire on your own time, Officer Daly. Get back to fucking work. You're not paid to gasbag on the street with every cunt in the country, now, are you?"

Jason's face turned a deep shade of scarlet, and he mumbled a response to his superior before bidding Finn a quick goodbye. Both officers took off in the direction they had first been headed without looking back.

"Could have saved your skin there, Finn. Where's Ollie?" Dominic asked sharply.

"Sick as a fuckin' dog, he is. I can manage without him just fine," Finn retorted sharply, his eyes shooting daggers at his uncle.

"See that you do. Manage, that is." And with that, Dominic rolled up the window and tore away.

"One of these days that prick will get what's coming to him," growled Finn. "He thinks I've forgotten what he did to my ma. To you. He'll get his."

His hands trembled with barely concealed anger, and unsure of what else to do, Megan grasped one and held it tightly in her own.

Shielding his eyes from the sun, Finn smiled at her, his face relaxing. He leaned forward and kissed her, gently first but then more passionately.

"Whatever would I do without you, Meg?"

"Well, you'll be happy to know that Daisy appears to be a perfectly healthy little girl. She may be a little out of sorts after her jabs, but that's perfectly normal. A little Calpol and Nurofen as the bottles direct will see her right as rain in no time at all."

The nurse, Franny, smiled down at the baby.

Daisy's face was red and scrunched up tight as she wailed in protest. Megan wanted to cry right alongside her daughter. The injections were a good thing in the long run, but it was so hard to see her child in discomfort.

Not to mention, time was running out and she hadn't figured out what to do yet.

"Would Daddy mind holding baby for just a moment while Mammy fills out a little form for me? I just need a quick rundown of how she's feeding, sleeping, etc. No offense to Daddy, but it's usually Mammy who knows these things." Franny smiled kindly at Finn as she took Daisy from Megan's arms and passed her across. "Come over here to me, love, and we'll get these filled out right quick."

Glancing at Finn, whose attention was turned entirely towards his grouchy daughter, Megan knew what she had to do.

Crossing the short space to the nurse's desk, she leaned over and started to fill in the questionnaire.

"You're American, Megan?" the nurse asked casually as she filled in her own notes beside her.

"Yes, Ma'am," Megan replied quietly. She could feel Finn's eyes on her. Without another word to the nurse, she carried on writing until the form was complete, then handed the sheet of paper across. Franny reached out to take it from her, and as their eyes met, Megan held her gaze for just a moment. She hoped the nurse was intuitive.

"So, we're good to go?" Finn asked, already standing and preparing to leave. He handed Daisy back to Megan. "Our son is at home, and he'll be anxious for us to get back."

"Yes, you can go ahead," Franny said.

Megan turned to look at the woman, but she was looking at her computer screen. The nurse had probably already mentally moved on to the next patient in her schedule. Megan knew she had likely just blown her chance at escape.

First those two guards. Now the nurse.

With a sigh of defeat, she turned to follow Finn from the room, cradling her daughter close to her chest and wondering how long she'd be able to protect her. She had let Daisy down monumentally.

"Just a minute, actually. The forms say Megan had a home birth. She probably hasn't been checked over since. Would you mind popping up there and letting me have a quick look at you, love?"

Her heart racing, Megan glanced up at Finn. Annoyance had spread over his features as he turned to face the nurse. "Is it really necessary? Like, right now?" he asked. "Couldn't we schedule another visit?"

The nurse's sunny disposition was replaced in an instant as she offered Finn a withering gaze. "Your wife's health is too important to reschedule. For the sake of five minutes, I'm sure you can wait outside."

The annoyance on Finn's face changed immediately to panic. "Outside?"

"Yes, outside. We do gynaecology examinations privately here, Mr Brogan."

"I was present during the birth of both of my children. I don't see why I need to leave for this."

"You need to leave because it is my office and my rules, Mr Brogan. I'm beginning to wonder why you are having such an issue understanding what I ask of you. This is a private examination, and for my and my patient's privacy, I ask that nobody be present in the room during said examination. Now, please, take a seat outside. The child can stay with her mother."

Knowing he was beat, Finn muttered to himself as he left the room. Megan watched him take a seat right outside the door. The nurse stalked across the room and closed the door, then turned concerned eyes on Megan. Guiding the younger woman by the arm, Franny moved them both across the room and into the cubicle. Megan sat heavily on the raised bed as Franny pulled the curtain around them.

"Tell me everything, love," Franny said, her eyes kind and compassionate.

And Megan did.

The words flooded from her in a river of tears and shame and anguish. She told her about Liam O'Keefe, about Ma who was also Lauren, about Tilly. She told her about the Brogan men, the words rushing out of her like an eruption of vomit. Through it all, as the past six years were purged from her, Franny sat quietly and listened. The only time the older woman showed any reaction was when Megan recounted the axe as it had fallen on her leg, chopping away her perfectly good limb and rendering her a cripple, unable to escape without huge hardship.

Even Daisy lay still, watching her mother through impossibly huge eyes, as though understanding the fate that could have befallen her. And when she was done, she was surprised to find that the tears had dried up alongside the words. She couldn't afford tears right now. She had saved her daughter, but she needed to save her son now too.

"I need to go out to the main desk and use the phone. Don't worry, I'll tell himself that I've found an infection and I'm just getting your prescription. I'll call the police from the back office." As she turned to leave, Megan grasped at her arm in panic, and Franny squeezed her shoulder in a comforting gesture. "Don't worry," she said. "I'll make sure his uncle doesn't know. I know Dominic Brogan. Never liked the man. And I know who his superior is. It just so happens that he's a friend of mine. I'll make sure they get to your boy before anyone tips that family off, love."

As the nurse left the room, Megan sagged against the bed. The curtain that still surrounded her was only thin linen, but in the moment, it felt like a steel barricade. It felt like it would keep her and Daisy safe from the beautiful monster outside the door.

Time dragged excruciatingly slowly. When the door opened, it felt like hours had passed. Megan's breath caught in her throat as a shape approached from the other side of the curtain. She was sure it was Finn. He had figured out what was happening. Nurse Franny had taken too long, and now he was coming to reclaim what was his before the world could tear them from him.

As the curtain pulled back, Megan flinched.

A soft hand on her arm quietened her galloping heart and Megan looked up at Franny with gratitude.

That gratitude died and ice flooded her veins as she noticed the nurse's grim expression.

"The guards are on their way, Megan. You and your daughter are safe now," Franny said gently. "But your husband is gone."

EPILOGUE: SURVIVAL INSTINCT

Megan sang softly as she rocked Daisy gently in her arms. The little girl's eyes fluttered once, twice, then dropped closed completely. Her breathing evened and tiny snorts indicated that she was finally asleep. With a heavy sigh, Megan shuffled awkwardly along the edge of the bed and placed her sleeping daughter gently into the crib. She was still learning to adjust to her new prosthetic, although she was getting better as each day passed. She was physically stronger, even if her bones were weary by the end of each day.

"Would you like to join us for a cuppa, Megan?"

Though the voice from the doorway was softly spoken, Megan still jumped just a little. She cursed her racing heart, wondering how long it would take for the nightmare to truly be over.

One of the other women who resided in the shelter stood in the doorway, her head tilted questioningly. Megan offered a small smile and shook her head.

"No, thanks, JoJo," she said for what felt like the millionth time.

The other girls in the women's shelter seemed lovely. Megan was surprised by how quickly she warmed to them.

When the dust had settled somewhat and she was finally allowed to leave the guard station, they brought her to this facility. She didn't think she would ever be able to trust another living soul after all she had been through, but she quickly recognised similar scars behind the eyes of the five women who shared this new home with her. Annie, JoJo, Angie, Patricia, and Marie were a friendly bunch, but there was a recognisable hesitance behind each action, every word. Nobody talked much about what had brought them there, yet some invisible thread connected them all, and shared pain had led to shared friendships. They were all survivors.

The women were all Irish except for Annie, who was a fellow American. It had surprised and delighted Megan to no end to meet someone from back home. She had connected with Annie more than the others, and nobody minded. The others had family and friends close by who visited, and they would all leave this place soon and return home to the arms of those who loved them. And Annie had loved ones waiting for her across the Atlantic. She knew Megan had nobody to return home to, so she insisted that she and Daisy accompany her to America, where her family would welcome them with open arms. They would happily accept the return of two daughters instead of one. But Megan knew she would never leave Ireland unless she was leaving with both of her children. The other women understood.

Still, she knew they whispered about what had happened to her.

Why wouldn't they?

When the authorities broke the story about her ordeal, it dominated national headlines for weeks. The international papers had run the story, too, although she faded to obscurity on a global scale pretty quickly.

Always a new story with more drama. More pain.

The Irish media had continued to carry the story, though, and old acquaintances of the Brogan family came forward with interview after interview.

Everybody was shocked.

Such a lovely family.

Good, hardworking men.

Maybe Megan was lying.

A woman scorned.

Even when the papers had leaked information about the personal effects that spanned decades.

The photographs.

The scattered bones that had been buried in the yard.

The dead girl in the basement.

Sometimes even the truth wasn't enough to tarnish what people thought they knew.

Her new therapist and the other women in the shelter advised her to avoid the media, but like a moth to a flame, Megan couldn't help herself.

Even though she had lived through it, she needed to ingest every single detail. The newspapers sensationalised the case so much that it almost felt as though the things that had actually happened became minimised in her mind. It almost made her chuckle on occasion.

Almost.

She scoured every article she could find, waiting for something that would point to Killian's whereabouts. So far, there had been nothing. No sightings.

Daisy was safe, and Megan thanked the universe every night for it. But a gaping hole still lived in her heart, and it would never be filled until she could save her baby boy from becoming a monster. He was so innocent. He didn't deserve to be a monster.

Didn't deserve to be a Brogan.

A gentle knock pulled her from her musings. She hadn't been aware of her tears, but now she could taste the salt as they traced a path along her cheeks. Megan wiped the last of them from her face, reached for her cane, and opened the door.

Annie stood there; her face wreathed in concern.

"I'm okay, Annie. Promise." Maybe a cup of tea and a chat was what she needed. She couldn't spend her life staring out of a different window. Wouldn't allow this to become a prison of her own making.

"There's a guard here to see you, Meg," Annie said solemnly. "He's in the kitchen. Go. I'll sit and watch over Daisy."

Megan shot her friend a grateful smile as she hobbled past her and headed for the kitchen. A visit meant news. Her heart soared at the prospect of information about Killian. For just a moment, she wouldn't allow herself to think about the potential for an unhappy outcome. Offering up a silent prayer to any god that cared to listen, she wished with every fibre of her being to be reunited with her son.

As she entered the kitchen and met the eye of the tall man in uniform, Megan's heart sank like a stone. Whatever news he had brought, she knew in an instant it wasn't good.

It was the soft cry of baby Daisy that drew Annie to the small bedroom next to hers. As she tiptoed across the soft carpet, she tried to ignore the knot in her stomach. She was worried about Megan.

After the police superintendent had left, Megan relayed his news with no emotion. The trail was cold. The case was still open, but for now, they had no leads to go on. Resources would be redeployed to other investigations.

Megan hadn't cried.

She hadn't screamed or raged.

She had simply stated that if the police couldn't find her son, then she would do it herself.

As the other women laughed together during dinner in the communal dining room, Annie eyed Megan. She sat stoically, nibbling at her food, smiling occasionally. But even a fool could tell that her mind was miles away with her little boy, wherever he was. Annie had tried to cajole her into talking some more. A problem shared was a problem halved, and all that. But Megan retired to her room early. She wanted to be alone.

And now it was the middle of the night, and Daisy was crying.

Stepping into the room, Annie's eyes were immediately drawn to the empty bed next to the crib. The covers were still neatly tucked.

Annie stole across the small space and looked into the crib.

Moonlight seeped through the thin curtains and bathed the little girl in a halo of ethereal light. She reached out and lifted Daisy, holding the small girl close to her chest and murmuring in her ear until the child's cries eased and she settled back into a deep slumber. Her body swayed slow and easy with the baby in her arms, but inwardly, Annie was panicking.

Megan was gone, and she needed to alert somebody.

Then she saw the slip of paper poking out from beneath the baby's pillow.

Lifting the note, Annie's eyes raced across the few scant lines on the page. With a small smile, she released a heavy breath and turned to leave. As she carried the baby back to her own room, she let the note flutter to the floor.

Megan had been through hell and back. She had a strong survival instinct, and Annie had no doubt that her new friend would return very soon.

And she wouldn't return alone.

The End

Author Notes

The Real Vanishing Triangle

This was a difficult book to write.

As a woman, it's never enjoyable to victimise my own gender, even if it is mere fiction.

It becomes exponentially more difficult when it's loosely tied to factual events.

People say I should use my platform to write strong female characters, and to that, I say, I have and I am. We can be victims and still be strong. Sometimes we make bad choices. Sometimes we make downright stupid choices. We fall for pretty lies and pretty faces. None of us are perfect. Many of us will be victims.

None of us deserve to be.

The women living in the shelter with Megan at the end of the book are all real victims. The Vanishing Triangle, as the Irish media have dubbed it, is very real. The lives lost there, some murdered, some missing, are very real.

All those stories led me to the loose outline of *Hush, My Darling*. It was a story waiting to be told. The mountains are so isolated and bad things happen there. I can see them from my back door. We used to drive through them frequently when I was a child to visit relatives, and I remember every single time, my ma would always wonder out loud about how many bodies must be buried there. What secrets they must contain within their isolated depths.

Truthfully, from the outset I had intended to feature the Vanishing Triangle more heavily than I did, but as I became invested in Megan and the other women, I couldn't bring myself to continue drawing upon that comparison. There is no entertainment in true crime, and to my mind, it is more terrifying than any subgenre of horror. Real people get hurt. Real people's lives are impacted. Real people are monsters.

So, I kept the thread of my story separate from the true stories of the Vanishing Triangle. There are families still grieving the loss of their mothers, sisters, daughters. There are families still waiting for their loved ones to come home. They don't know the pain of death, and they also don't know the kindness of closure. They're stuck in purgatory. In their own personal version of Hell.

And so, I decided to use some of the victims' names for the women in the shelter with Megan. In my fictional reality, they are safe. They will return home to their loved ones.

They are survivors.

From the moment I first outlined the story in my head, Megan was supposed to die. I never intended for her to live, but her character took over. She became her own person and insisted on beating the odds. She didn't give up on her children. She didn't give up on herself. If that isn't a strong female character, then I don't know what is.

Megan is a survivor.

We are survivors.

For further reading on Ireland's Vanishing Triangle, I recommend checking out Irish journalist Sarah McInerney's book *Where No One Can Hear You Scream: Murder and Assault in the Wicklow Mountains.*

In Memory of Ted

He was the goodest of good doggos.

The chocolate Labrador in this story is based on my dog, Ted. The description is him, the behaviour is him, and sadly, the final scene is his too. And mine.

I had Ted for fourteen amazing years, and while I'll never get over the devastation I felt watching him take his final breaths, I'll always be glad that the last face he looked upon was the one he cherished throughout his doggy life. He left a hole in my heart when he passed, and this book has ensured that he will live on forever in some form. That thought brings me no end of comfort.

Run free, Teddy Bear.

Acknowledgements

I promise that this section will be MUCH shorter than the last one. IYKYK!

I have to start by acknowledging my wonderful partner. He shows nothing but encouragement and patience as I navigate this whole author thing. I couldn't do it without you, Wig.

My boys, Kyran and Odhran, who contribute nothing to my writing but everything to my soul. May you never experience any horror in your lives except for the words I write.

My mother always gets a mention because she is the most amazing person I know. I am a strong woman because I was raised by an even stronger woman.

I am lucky to be blessed with so many wonderful people in my life: Casey, Shauna, Thomas, Gran, Da, Dayna . . . I love you all.

Sarah Jules and MJ Mars, my sassy squad, you keep me sane daily. I would genuinely be lost without your friendship.

Matt Rayner, you are one of my favourite people, even though you did tell everyone that I wrote a book about cursed pubes.

Ben Young and Chris Jones, two of my biggest supporters in the industry. Give it a little time and I'll be riding on both your coattails!

My editor, Danielle Yeager, who has the patience of a saint and the eyes of an eagle. She makes it all make sense. My cover designer, Christy Aldridge, for knocking it out of the park once more. My beta readers, especially Barry Hollywood, for his unrivalled attention to detail. My ARC readers for being fantastic and honest and gentle with me. The Books of Horror group on Facebook for being such an amazing and supportive space for horror authors and horror readers alike.

And finally, the biggest acknowledgement of all goes to you, dear reader. Without you, there would still be a book, but nobody would care. Every word you read, every book you review, every positive interaction we have . . . it all means the world. I'm so happy we're on this journey together.

ABOUT THE AUTHOR

Leigh was born and raised in the garden county of Wicklow, Ireland. She lives by the Irish Sea with the love of her life, two wonderful boys, a black Labrador, and a three-legged cat that hates people. You can find out more about Leigh's work and any upcoming releases on her social media: LeighKennyWrites

ALSO BY LEIGH KENNY

Novellas:

Cursed

Featured Anthologies:

Books of Horror Community Anthology Vol. 4 Pt.2

Screams From the Ocean Floor

Final Passenger

The Horror Collection: Book 19

Scorned

Books of Horror Indie Brawl Anthology

Printed in Dunstable, United Kingdom